PROFILE

FIRSTBORN SON:	Sheik Rashid Kamal
AGE:	37
STATS:	6'1"; short, conservatively cut raven hair; shrewd dark eyes; tall, athletic build; handsome, exotic features
OCCUPATION:	Crown Prince of the Kingdom of Tamir
AREA OF EXPERTISE:	International diplomacy (and seduction!)
PERSONALITY:	Charmingly arrogant on the surface, Rashid is an intensely passionate man who cares deeply about life, and is determined to bring peace to his country.
FAVORITE SPORTS:	Polo and sailing
MOST CHARMING CHARACTERISTIC:	When he finally does fall in love, he's a one-woman man.
BRAVEST ACT OF COURAGE:	Challenging the terrorist group known as the Brothers of Darkness—and winning
PREFERRED ROMANTIC SETTING:	His fabulous private Greek island
GREATEST PASSION:	Trying to convince a certain pregnant princess that marriage with him is the best way out of her dilemma

Dear Reader,

Happy (almost) New Year! The year is indeed ending, but here at Intimate Moments it's going out with just the kind of bang you'd expect from a line where excitement is the order of the day. Maggie Shayne continues her newest miniseries, THE OKLAHOMA ALL-GIRL BRANDS, with *Brand-New Heartache*. This is prodigal daughter Edie's story. She's home from L.A. with a stalker on her trail, and only local one-time bad boy Wade Armstrong can keep her safe. Except for her heart, which is definitely at risk in his presence.

Our wonderful FIRSTBORN SONS continuity concludes with *Born Royal*. This is a sheik story from Alexandra Sellers, who's made quite a name for herself writing about desert heroes, and this book will show you why. It's a terrific marriage-of-convenience story, and it's also a springboard for our twelve-book ROMANCING THE CROWN continuity, which starts next month. Kylie Brant's *Hard To Resist* is the next in her CHARMED AND DANGEROUS miniseries, and this steamy writer never disappoints with her tales of irresistible attraction. *Honky-Tonk Cinderella* is the second in Karen Templeton's HOW TO MARRY A MONARCH miniseries, and it's enough to make any woman want to run away and be a waitress, seeing as this waitress gets to serve a real live prince. Finish the month with Mary McBride's newest, *Baby, Baby, Baby,* a "No way am I letting my ex-wife go to a sperm bank" book, and reader favorite Lorna Michaels's first Intimate Moments novel, *The Truth About Elyssa.*

See you again next year!

Leslie J. Wainger
Executive Senior Editor

Please address questions and book requests to:
Silhouette Reader Service
U.S.: 3010 Walden Ave., P.O. Box 1325, Buffalo, NY 14269
Canadian: P.O. Box 609, Fort Erie, Ont. L2A 5X3

BORN ROYAL

Alexandra Sellers

Silhouette®

INTIMATE MOMENTS™

Published by Silhouette Books

America's Publisher of Contemporary Romance

Special thanks and acknowledgment are given
to Alexandra Sellers for her contribution
to the FIRSTBORN SONS series.
For Michael Hunter Lewis Sellers Fairweather
my incomparable, much-loved nephew and godson
who is also a firstborn son
U donad, U donad, U donad—U!
(He knows, He knows, He knows—He!)
—from the *Rubaiyat* of Omar Khayyam

SILHOUETTE BOOKS

RECYCLED PAPER

ISBN 0-373-27188-3

BORN ROYAL

Bound by the legacy of their fathers, six Firstborn Sons are about to discover the stuff true heroes—and true love—are made of....

Sheik Rashid Kamal: To bring peace and prosperity to Montebello and Tamir, Prince Rashid must unite the Kamal and Sebastiani kingdoms. First order of business—pull out *all* the stops to claim the pregnant Princess Julia as his enamored bride. Let the games begin!

Princess Julia Sebastiani: Sheik Rashid Kamal is a dangerously attractive enemy for whom she has already proven she has a fatal weakness. Now the high-handed prince has gone *too* far by making a public marriage declaration without her consent! This willful princess will wed for love—or not at all....

Sheik Ahmed Kamal: As he rejoices in his heroic son's triumphant return home, he realizes it won't be long before Rashid receives the throne. But for now, a peaceful trade treaty between Montebello and Tamir must be forged. And to further that agenda, the mysterious origin of their bitter animosity needs to be unraveled.

The Noble Men: Over the years, they have taken calculated risks and sacrificed their own personal happiness to achieve their global pursuits. Has the time finally come to pass their legacy on to their firstborn sons?

A note from beloved author Alexandra Sellers:

Dear Reader,

I was delighted to be invited to write the final book in the Intimate Moments FIRSTBORN SONS series. It's the first continuity I've taken part in, and I found it both difficult and exciting. I have really enjoyed collaborating with the other writers in the series, especially Virginia Kantra. Virginia and I co-wrote scenes in each of our books between the two princess sisters, Julia and Christina. That was good fun.

Born Royal is my thirtieth novel for Harlequin/ Silhouette, and my eleventh sheikh fantasy. Readers familiar with me know that my passion for all things Middle Eastern dates back to my early childhood, when, in the tiny prairie town where I spent a very difficult two years, I discovered a book called *The Arabian Nights*. I began to dream of flying carpets, handsome princes and genies in magic lamps. I've never stopped.

Since then I have traveled to some of those places I dreamed of, and have been privileged to explore, a little, their languages and religion, history and wisdom. It is a world as deep, as rich and as many-layered as that magical book—which I still treasure—promised me it would be. I hope that in my own stories I am able to communicate to you some part of the fascination and wonder of the East that has enchanted me and enriched my life for so long.

Alexandra Sellers

Prologue

Prince Rashid ibn Ahmed Kamal stood on the broad balcony of the palace smiling and waving as the love-roar of the crowd swelled almost to pain level and broke over his head.

Below the balcony, the huge, leafy square writhed ecstatically in the burning sunshine as the people cheered, shouted, laughed, sang, danced and kissed each other.

He was home. Their handsome Crown Prince, whom they had mourned as lost forever, had returned. And better still, he had returned a hero. As the man who had organized and masterminded the downfall of that band of murderous terrorists, the one so fearful no one liked to say its full name, but only called them *Al Ikhwan*. The Brothers.

Now the people need not live in fear of the threatened chemical attack. It was said he had found the actual laboratory where the filthy poisons were being made, and that the entire store of the evil virus had been destroyed.

No one needed to be told where the first attack would

have occurred. But a country storyteller, who had a sizable group entranced with his version of the prince's great exploit, told them anyway.

"Of course they would have attacked here in the islands of Tamir first," he asserted in a terrible voice, and his audience gasped and nodded. "Such monsters as these are drawn to destroy truth and nobility, for they know instinctively there is no co-existence between evil and good.

"And for a certainty they would have come here, to the big island—and to this city, Medina Tamir. Perhaps even in this very square they would have released their foul poison, hoping to destroy the Kamal family and put their own puppet in Ahmed's place!"

His audience of mostly city dwellers shuddered in horrified delight. The country people had a point—this was much more entertaining than the dry facts in newspapers or on television.

"And only when we died would the world have been alerted and begun to take action," the turbaned, white-bearded ancient said, conveniently omitting the fact that the mission Prince Rashid had headed had been a joint one involving many nations. "Too late for Tamir. But what need have we of the world, when we have a prince such as Rashid? Brave, intrepid..."

The cheers redoubled as Prince Rashid was joined on the balcony by the rest of his family. The silver-haired King Ahmed, lovely Queen Alima, handsome Prince Hassan and his sisters, the beautiful and headstrong Princess Nadia, gentle, smiling Samira, and Leila—the youngest and, some argued, the loveliest.

It was Nadia who stood closest to Rashid as the family took their places, smiling and waving to the delirious citizenry. She glanced down at the crowd around the storyteller in the square, and pointed him out to her brother.

"By the end of the week you'll have done the deed single-handed," she remarked in an ironic aside. "Flying on the back of a giant bird, the Natobird, no doubt, and with the sword of your ancestors—I suppose they'll call it the Kalashnikov sword—raised high, you dispatched the monsters after a fight to the death and won your way to the coffers wherein lay the terrible poison. You threw magical powder on the poison to render it harmless."

Rashid laughed, not because she wasn't right in her analysis. Nadia had an instinctive understanding of people and events, and it was a pity his father didn't consult her more often in matters of state.

"Well, and if my mythical powers win the people to my side when I'm proposing a shift in foreign policy, among other things, I won't object."

Nadia flicked him a look. He should have known she would be quick to pick up on that hint. "Other things? As for example?"

Rashid shook his head, turning to lift his hand again and smile. The sun was high in the blue sky, burnishing the thick black curls, enhancing the glint in his dark eyes and the white, even teeth. The crowd swayed with reaction.

There was no one, Nadia reflected, whom he did not, one way or another, seduce. He had much more charisma than their rather severe father. It was no wonder that the people had been brokenhearted when Rashid went missing.

As for her, it had been like losing a limb. The miracle of having her brother back from the dead had not worn off yet. Maybe it never would.

"'Among other things,'" Nadia repeated musingly, sliding an arm through her brother's. "Now, what else would you be *proposing* besides a shift in foreign policy?" He was silent. "So the baby really is yours? I wondered."

His gaze turning inward, Prince Rashid absently waved

and smiled. The crowd cheered. He thought of Julia's soft cry when his hands were on her, when what was going to happen was inevitable. *Rashid, I'm—I'm a virgin....*

He had not believed her. Other women had said it to him at such a moment; he had never understood why. Hoping to make his passion hotter, perhaps.

But it was true. When he realized it, too late, it had struck him a blow like nothing else he had experienced. A virgin. After all this time, she was a virgin.

"Yes, it's mine," he said.

He thought of the way she had melted at his touch, saw her face in his mind's eye, those full lips stretched with desire. He had lost control.

"It will put an end to the feud, won't it?" Nadia commented. "If marriage is what's in your mind."

Had it been his unconscious mind understanding that the one unanswerable way to bind them together was a child? Was that the reason such powerful desire had swept him, blinding him to every other consideration? His one chance offered, and he had taken it.

"The question is, what's the best way of getting Father over the hump?" Rashid murmured. "He's not going to like it, is he?"

Nadia laughed outright at the understatement. "The feud is what keeps him going, you know that."

There was another round of cheers from below as their father and mother turned back inside the palace.

"I don't want a war with him. But I have to do what I know to be right. If I could find a way to make him accept it—" He shrugged and waved to the crowds again as his sisters and brother left.

"Want some advice, big brother?"

Now there were only Nadia and Rashid. They waved a last farewell as the crowds went crazy with cheering.

"Yes, I want advice."

"Play it the same way you played your last enterprise." Nadia smiled and flicked her raised hand at him. "Surprise him."

Chapter 1

Princess Julia Sebastiani twitched awake, her heart pounding, sweat on her forehead. She lay without moving, wondering where she was, as the memory of pleasure subsided in her blood. After a moment she sighed. She was in her bedroom at the palace. Alone.

The clock across the room read 6:30. Well, that was more sleep than she usually got when she dreamt of Rashid Kamal. She struggled to a sitting position and dropped her face in her hands. It was no use to try to get back to sleep; she had learned that through experience.

She slipped off the bed, crossed the room to the windows that looked southeast, and stood there, gazing out at the sun rising in splendour out of the Mediterranean Sea. It was a view she had loved all her life, but even in childhood her pleasure had been coloured by the knowledge that in that direction, over the horizon, out of sight, lay Tamir.

He was home. He was alive. Her child had a father—who was the son of her own father's sworn enemy.

She had never known whether to think him alive or dead. Sometimes she had wondered if it had all been a plot to cast doubt on the Sebastianis—if Rashid Kamal had set it all up, the unexpected meeting, the surprised passion, and then his disappearance, so that the Sebastianis would be suspected in his disappearance just as the Kamals were suspected in the loss of her brother, Lucas. Other times she had despaired, sure that he was dead and that her son would all his life bear the stigma of belonging to a family suspected of killing his father.

He must know by now that she was pregnant. She wondered if he accepted that he was the father of her child. There was so much accusation and counter-accusation between the Kamals and the Sebastianis that it would hardly be surprising if he did not.

Julia and Prince Rashid to Marry!
A Montebello Messenger *World Exclusive!*
Crown Prince Rashid of Tamir and Princess Julia will marry "as soon as it can be arranged," the *Montebello Messenger* has learned. In an exclusive interview with this reporter, the heir to the throne of Tamir, whose family has maintained a long-standing and well-publicized feud with Montebello's own royal family, said that he felt the ill feeling between the two families was "a thing of the past" which should be forgotten.

"A man and woman cannot carry on an ancient feud when they are about to have a child together," he said. "My interest is not in the past, but in the future. It is time to look ahead, to a time of peace between our two countries."

The prince confirmed unequivocally that he is the father of Princess Julia's child, a question about which there has been intense media speculation since his unexpected return from the dead early this week.

The palace here in Montebello has not so far responded to Rashid's claims that a wedding between the Crown Prince and Princess Julia is in the offing.

"Damn you! Damn you!" Julia flung the *Montebello Messenger* to the floor with a cry of disbelief.

"Ma—madame?" a voice trembled behind her.

In the mirror her hairdresser's face looked startled and wary.

"Oh—Micheline! Not you! Sorry!" she said, forcing a smile. She had never felt less like smiling in her life.

The paper landed with the front page up, and Rashid's beard-shadowed face grinned at her, black grease smudged on his cheekbone and forehead. His eyes seemed to mock her even from a distance of ten feet. Behind him was a military helicopter. In one hand he held an assault rifle.

The hairdresser's eyes followed hers. "'E is veree 'andsome, madame," she said shyly.

Until this moment, none of her staff had had the nerve to mention in her presence the one subject that was on everyone's mind, though Julia knew it was about all they discussed behind her back.

"Who is?" the princess snapped, in her mother's best *we-are-not-amused* tone.

But Micheline was just too thrilled by this latest turn of events in the months-long drama the world had been following with such excitement. Who could have kept silent now?

"But the prince, madame!" she supplied breathlessly. *"Et quel héros! Si brave!"* She slipped into her native French, English being insufficient for her feelings. "To conquer those terrorists, madame! To risk his life to save us from the anthrax…" She sighed luxuriously. "I am sure you are very happy, madame. Who would not be, with such a man to love her?''

Julia pressed her lips together and made no reply. She might almost have been fooled by the romance of it herself, if she hadn't known better. She couldn't understand what game he was playing. But that it was a game was certain.

''Everyone is so happy, madame, to know that you will be happy at last!''

Julia's jaw clenched. Whatever this latest move meant, it boded no happiness for her. Happy? With a man whose family was still manipulating a painful, century-old tragedy into a totally unjustified claim on Sebastiani land?

''So, madame, what do you think?'' Micheline prompted, unabashed. It was a moment before Julia realized that she was being urged to admire her own hair.

Julia no longer wore the smooth pleat that had once almost been her trademark. This morning her long, dark hair had been loosely caught back, with soft curling tendrils escaping all around her head.

The style emphasized the fine bones of her face, very prominent now because of the weight she had lost over the past year, the porcelain skin, the wide blue eyes. She was starting to gain the weight back now, with the pregnancy, but she was still much thinner than she had been in those days when her marriage had seemed storybook perfect from the outside.

''Perfect, Micheline, thank you,'' the princess said, her smile reflected in the deep blue eyes in a way that ensured that most of her staff would walk across burning coals if she asked them to. She got to her feet just as her chief private secretary came through the door, a sheaf of papers in one arm, an extremely odd look on her face.

''Valerie,'' said Julia, as Micheline brushed her down,

"have you seen that?" She indicated the newspaper on the floor, and Valerie stopped short and bent to pick it up.

A stupid question at nearly 9:00 am. The entire island had read or heard the story by now.

"Uh—yes," Valerie replied blankly.

"Will you tell Bertrand I want to talk to him? Immediately, please, if he can make it."

"I'm sure he's waiting to talk to you," Valerie said, pulling out her phone.

Micheline handed Julia into her jacket. The soft dusty rose suit had a pencil skirt—she could still wear those—but the boxy jacket hung low over her hips, disguising the first signs of her pregnancy. Underneath she wore a neat white bodysuit with a low scooped neck. She slipped on gold medallion earrings as Micheline passed them to her. On her wrist she wore the bracelet of gold and diamonds she called her lucky bracelet.

"Thanks, Micheline," Julia said, with another smile.

Valerie meanwhile was talking to Bertrand, passing on her message. She disconnected as Julia took the newspaper from her hand.

"He'll meet us," Valerie said, and the two women left the room to stride down the hall together.

Although obviously consumed with curiosity, Valerie calmly began her usual briefing. "You've got the Arts Council representatives due at nine-thirty. I'll put them in the Blue Room. They'll be asking…"

Julia tried to concentrate, but the world seemed to be behind a veil. It was happening more and more lately—no doubt it was pregnancy hormones. She just didn't seem to have the attack, or the cool nerves, she was known for.

Or maybe it was because she was preoccupied with what Rashid Kamal had said to the media. What game was he playing? Everyone knew a Sebastiani could never marry a Kamal, baby on the way or not. Even if she wanted to.

Which Julia certainly did not. Marry a Kamal? Not if he was the last man standing.

Bertrand, in a smart blue suit and collarless shirt, was waiting in the anteroom of Julia's private offices, one hand in his pocket, looking rather irritated. They all moved through to the inner office.

Julia tossed the newspaper down on a low table in the centre of a cluster of chairs and sofas before seating herself and waving at them to do the same.

"You've read it, Bertrand?"

Of course he had. As her press secretary he made it his business to see everything printed about her, usually before Julia did. He and Valerie slipped into seats facing hers on either side and he leaned forward and picked up the *Montebello Messenger,* looked at it, then at her.

"Yes, I got my own copy, as usual. May I say—"

"He's got one hell of a nerve! I wonder what he's playing at?"

Bertrand, his head bent, elbows on knees, lifted his gaze and looked at her under his brows in silent astonishment.

"I'd like to issue a statement as soon as possible, please."

The press secretary paused, as if waiting for more. Then he prompted, "What do you want me to say, Princess?"

"A categorical denial that there's any engagement or any possibility of a marriage, of course!"

"It's not true?"

"I wish these—what?" She jumped as if her seat were suddenly electrified. "True? No, of course it's not true! Are you crazy, Bertrand?"

His mouth relaxed imperceptibly. "Forgive me, Princess. I assumed the two of you had—"

"Had what?" Julia stared at him, and realized belatedly that Bertrand thought she had gone behind his back to make this announcement with Rashid. He had probably been mentally drafting up his letter of resignation, which was just one more sin to lay at Rashid Kamal's door.

"Rashid Kamal is a Kamal. He is a long-standing enemy of the Sebastiani family, and that includes myself. I haven't spoken to him since his return."

Bertrand nodded, one eyebrow raised.

"Has Papa seen it? Has he called?" Her father and mother, thank God, were abroad this week. "He must be raving."

"I understand that he has called. He did not speak to me," her press secretary said carefully.

Julia almost laughed. "Well, and you're grateful for that! Why didn't he ask to speak to me?"

"I understand he has left a number and hopes that you will call when you have a moment."

"That bad, huh?" Julia smiled, but inwardly she quailed a little. Her father would be in a towering rage until she could explain.

"I can't believe the *Messenger* ran the story without calling us for a reaction! Why didn't they check with us first?" she demanded furiously.

"Because what the prince said will sell papers," Bertrand told her dryly. "Our reaction, which they hope to run in the later editions, will sell more copies. Prince Rashid has timed it very nicely. The *Messenger* is probably going to break all previous sales records today. And given the last few months, that's saying something."

"Well, make getting the statement out your first priority this morning. And I suppose I'd better make Papa mine."

"Princess, if I may make a suggestion..."

She looked an inquiry.

"I'd like to suggest that we refuse to comment for the moment."

Julia stared. "You want me to *refuse to comment* on a story that says I'm going to marry Rashid Kamal?" she repeated with slow precision. "Are you out of your *mind?*"

She felt the baby's whisper of protest as adrenaline pumped into her blood. Julia paused, her hand automatically moving to her abdomen. She stroked for a moment and took a deep calming breath.

"Okay, Bertrand." Julia's other hand lifted gracefully, the palm pressing outward, as if to hold back the wave she felt coming towards her. Julia glanced at Valerie. "What's your point?"

"Princess, all hell has broken loose this morning, which is no surprise. My private line alone has already logged over a hundred calls from journalists. We've had to call in half a dozen relief staff for the palace switchboard to cope with calls from citizens. And this is only a trickle compared with what's to come," Bertrand told her.

"Then the sooner we issue a statement, the better, surely?"

"We're even getting calls from Tamiri citizens."

"Screaming how appalled they are, I'm sure!"

"No. For once, Montebello and Tamir have synoptic vision on an issue. The truth is, Princess, everybody wants to believe it."

Julia sucked in too much air too suddenly and started coughing. When the fit was over she stared at her press secretary.

"The citizens of both countries are thrilled at the prospect of a marriage that will put an end to this feud once and for all," he informed her. "As a public relations coup, on top of the military action, it's pretty damned good. He knows his stuff, Rashid."

This made her furious.

"No doubt. I don't know what Rashid Kamal has in mind, but he means us no good, you can be sure. No Kamal can be trusted." She had a sudden sharp memory of his black eyes, burning into hers. *Kiss me. Kiss me.*

Valerie leaned forward. "Are you absolutely certain that he isn't serious? It's an extraordinary risk to take if he's not. Where would he be if you publicly said yes?"

A little shock went through her. "Are you suggesting— no. No, of course he's not serious! A Kamal marry a Se-bastiani? Impossible!"

Valerie and Bertrand looked at her oddly. But neither wanted to be the one to point out a more impossible fact— that a Kamal had made a Sebastiani pregnant.

"I imagine the point of this exercise—" she waved at the newspaper "—is that Rashid Kamal gets to look like a knight in shining armour. I'm pregnant. He offers marriage. I turn him down. He's squeaky clean."

Her conscience tugged at her a little as she spoke. The Kamals had been characterized as monsters all her life, but Rashid had not seemed like that to her when she met him. If he hadn't been a Kamal, she would even have called him… But her mind wouldn't go there.

"Wouldn't it be wiser to find out for certain what's in his mind before we jump to any action? Everyone's been very worried and stressed lately, Princess, afraid that an-other bomb was going to go off, or they'd be inhaling poi-son in the streets. It's not going to hurt them to feel for a few hours that they've seen the end of animosity and the beginning of peace."

Julia eyed Bertrand suspiciously, wondering what was in his mind.

"I don't accept that the majority of the citizens of this country or of Tamir are rejoicing in the thought of such a marriage, however many calls there have been. But if they are, Bertrand, recollect that it is I who will tear this cup from their lips when the moment finally comes. I'd like to do that sooner rather than later."

Bertrand gave her a steady look. "With respect, Princess, you'll need to talk to Prince Rashid. I could start the ball rolling by calling my opposite number at the palace."

"I'm not going to talk to him," Julia said, keeping her voice as level as she could.

"Princess, that's crazy. You—"

Julia got to her feet, catching the other two off guard. They scrambled to follow.

"All right, Bertrand, you can call the palace in Tamir," she said. "And tell Prince Rashid from me that if he says any more about this supposed marriage to the media or anyone else, I'll...he'll..."

The threat, if it was one, was interrupted. There was a hurried knock, and then the office door burst open. One of the junior secretaries came in, wide-eyed and almost babbling with poorly suppressed excitement.

"I'm sorry, Your Highness, but I thought I should— um...they've just notified me that he's here! He's actually in the palace. Prince Rashid! And he—he wants to see you!"

"Bertrand, go down to him, please," Julia commanded, in a low, trembling voice he had to strain to hear. "Will you explain that we are going to issue an unqualified denial of this story, and ask that he support that with a statement of his own."

"Princess, wouldn't it be better—" Bertrand began.

"No, it wouldn't!" she cried, feeling goaded beyond her endurance. "Allow me to be the judge, please! Tell him whatever you like about why. Just make it very clear that *I am not going to see him.*"

"Predicting the future is a risky business," chided a deep masculine voice from the open doorway. Julia, Bertrand, Valerie and the junior secretary all whirled.

In the doorway, beside an embarrassed and apologetic member of King Marcus's staff, stood Rashid Kamal, smiling like an angel of vengeance.

"See? Wrong already," he said.

Chapter 2

They both stood silent, half the width of the room between them, gazing at each other. Those watching the pair felt a curious sensation, as if they themselves, and the room, had somehow ceased to exist in the same reality.

Rashid's mocking smile died as he took in the sight of her. He wondered when her face had become his icon of survival. There had been times in the past few months when he'd come up against the real possibility that he wouldn't succeed in his mission, wouldn't even survive it. He realized only now how often in those moments his thoughts had been of Julia. Julia and his child.

Julia licked her lips and swallowed. A huge relief flooded her, taking her completely by surprise. He was alive. Until this moment she hadn't realized how much of a tragedy it would have been if he were not.

As if embarrassed to be intruding, the others began to shuffle uncomfortably. Reality suddenly returned. Their gaze unlocked.

"We have things to discuss," Rashid said, entering the room and acknowledging the staff in one friendly but imperious nod. With wonderful noblesse oblige, he held the door for them to leave. And to Julia's annoyance, her staff all instinctively obeyed, leaving her alone with the enemy.

A dangerously attractive enemy, for whom she was already proven to have a fatal weakness. With whom she had made a total, complete, and utter fool of herself. She shifted uncomfortably, then reminded herself where she was. This was her own private office.

"Are the Kamals now laying claim to this palace, as well as Delia's Land?" she demanded with icy sarcasm.

Rashid looked at her in level scrutiny, ignoring her outburst. He took a step closer. "How are you, Julia?" She seemed well, with softer curves than when he had last seen her. But the shadow in her eyes as she looked at him was the same.

The scent of her perfume was a sudden, sharp reminder of that wild night when passion had nearly wrecked all his careful plans. In the months since, he had found ways to explain what had happened. His reaction had been a simple side effect of the dangerous enterprise he had been about to embark upon, he had told himself. Men going to war had always been prey to such reactions—the universal unconscious compulsion to leave some trace of his genes in the world before he left it had seized him, that was all.

But that did not explain his reaction to her now—the need to hold her, to wrap her in safety. He reached for her with impatient arms.

She stepped back, evading his embrace.

"All the worse for seeing you!" she retorted.

Rashid's head snapped back as if a cat had scratched his cheek without warning.

"The *worse* for seeing me? Why?"

"Why did you tell that *Messenger* journalist we were engaged?" she demanded.

"The real reason?"

"Of course, the real reason!"

"I thought there was a chance it would go over better with your people if I gave the exclusive to a Montebello paper. I've heard it's going down very well."

Julia gritted her teeth. "You know perfectly well what I mean! What did you say it for? What's your agenda?"

He frowned. "What's yours?"

She wasn't sure why she was so furious suddenly. "My agenda? That's simple—to have a baby. With the least possible media intrusion on the event, if you wouldn't mind!"

"There'll be a lot less room for speculation and innuendo once we're married."

Julia jerked backwards as if he had burned her. She opened her mouth twice, like a fish. "Married?" she whispered faintly. "What—you—we can't get married!"

The sparkle abruptly left his dark eyes. He had hoped—he had felt almost certain of her support in his plans, if no one else's.

"Can't we?"

Julia bit her lip and gazed at him, trying to figure him out. She had been convinced what he had done was merely another move in some elaborate game plan. A game plan in which she was a pawn who would be sacrificed when necessary.

"You seriously imagine that we might get married?"

He watched her, his dark eyes unreadable. She still didn't believe it. She wished he would tell her what he really wanted. This was making her very uncomfortable.

"Why not?"

"Your name is Kamal. Mine is Sebastiani."

"We managed to make a baby, nevertheless."

Julia's cheeks burned at this calculated reminder of what she had let happen. "Everybody's allowed to go out of their tiny mind once."

"Is that what you call it?"

"What do you call it?" she challenged.

He looked at her. Looked at the rich dark hair, the delicate skin moulding fine bones, the wide mouth that seemed to tremble with the passage of every feeling. Her long neck holding her head like a flower on a stem, and the soft, fresh skin of her throat. The slender body, with its high, lush breasts, fuller now than what his hands remembered. The slim hips, curving thighs, fine ankles. Shoes to match her suit and her pink mouth.

His examination left her shaking with a kind of fury.

"I call it going out of my tiny mind," he admitted. "But why only once?"

She swallowed, her eyes widening at the implication. "You—" she began, half-panicked.

He stepped forward with his hands outstretched to grip her arms. Julia avoided the touch by backing up. Her knees bumped up against the sofa, and she sat down with less grace than she was known for. He stood looking down at her, his eyes dark and assessing. She moved her shoulders nervously.

"You are pregnant with my child. You must have been expecting this."

"Expecting an offer of marriage?" she repeated disbelievingly. "From the man whose father used every opportunity to accuse me of having slept with you in order to murder you? I'm afraid not!"

She stiffened as Rashid sank down beside her. "I am sorry," he said. "But you must see I had no control over this. We were working to stop the Brothers of Darkness.

There was nothing I could do to set the record straight, without jeopardizing the whole enterprise.''

"Set the record straight? Why would you do that?'' she cried. "You'd worked so hard to get me where I was!''

"Worked?'' he repeated with a half smile. "You really were a virgin, weren't you? That wasn't work, Julia.''

She bit her lip as humiliation flooded her. What a fool she had made of herself with him. And how cruel of him to mock her.

"And how could I have known that you would get pregnant?''

"You knew damned well you were going to disappear that night, though, didn't you?''

"Yes, I did.''

"Yes. And you arranged it so that I was the last person to see you 'alive.' I wonder if you can imagine what's it's like to have some very polite police detectives asking you in the kindest terms about the feud your families have been waging for the past century and how strongly you feel about it!''

"It was no part of my plan to incriminate you. Is that what you've been thinking? No. It was completely wrong of me to—'' he paused and reached out a finger to stroke back a tendril of hair from her temple "—to allow myself to make love to you. But you know what inducement I had, Julia.''

"Inducement? I never—''

His voice changed, turning into a seductive growl as he reminded them both. His fingers caught the delicate curl of her hair, stopping her as she tried to move her head away.

The memory of his touch rippled over her skin.

"You were irresistible. So beautiful. You called my name, and I was lost.''

She struggled to subdue the heat his voice summoned up

in her. She could not bear it if he made her look a fool
again.

"If it hadn't been for Lucas's d-disappearance..." Julia
choked. She felt the tears burn again, undermining her.
Even now she could not say the word. Like her father, she
couldn't apply the word *death* to Lucas.

She burned with humiliation. "Yes, all right, I threw
myself at you! But if Lucas...if I hadn't been so distraught
over my brother, you wouldn't have got near me," she
finished.

"It should not have happened," Rashid agreed, with an
edge to his otherwise calm voice. "But it did happen, and
we are left with the results. What is the benefit in arguing
over how we got where we are? The important thing
now—"

"It might help to clear the air!" Julia exclaimed.

"Damn it, what is unclear?"

"What is unclear is what can be feeding your delusion
that we are going to get married! Or what you thought gave
you the right to undermine me with the announcement of
our engagement!"

"*Undermine* you? Julia, I came home to a barrage of
media speculation that I was going to repudiate you and
your claim to be carrying my child. My first thought was
to protect you from any suspicion that I doubted your child
was mine."

"Your first thought was to get Delia's Land," she corrected him. "I suppose it was to please your father."

Prince Rashid abruptly lost his grip on his calm. "How
dare you accuse me of this? You must know that my father
was distraught over my disappearance—too distraught to
be rational. Your own father has expressed his sufferings
in the same unintelligent way!"

"My father at least never used his grief as an excuse to grab Tamir land—"

"Your father accused my father of masterminding your brother's disappearance," he interrupted ruthlessly. "Also of planting bombs and orchestrating the kidnap attempts on you and your sister. What was this, if not an attempt to undermine my father's reign, distance his allies and assist the *Ikhwan al Zalaam*—the Brothers of Darkness—in their bid to unseat us?"

His voice flicked her like a whip.

"There was good reason to suspect the Kamals!" she cried. "One bomber even confessed he'd been hired by your father! What would you expect my father to think?"

"The bomber lied. It was deliberate disinformation," Rashid informed her levelly, as if she didn't already know. "And I would expect from your father what I would expect from any intelligent person in a position of power—a calm and reasoned response to something that could easily have provoked a crisis."

"Like King Ahmed's, I suppose! Waiting till my father's beside himself over Lucas and then demanding Delia's Land again."

They were almost shouting. He realized, not for the first time, how little self-control he had around her.

Rashid shook his head in exasperation. "Julia, can't you understand that what Delia's Land represents to my father isn't land, but a sense of closure, of justice? Rightly or wrongly, a century ago the Kamal family believed that their Crown Prince was murdered by the Sebastianis. In their view they were entitled—"

Julia flared up. Nothing was more certain to get Sebastiani blood hot than a repetition of this stupid, baseless accusation. Tamir's Crown Prince Omar Kamal and Montebello's Princess Delia Sebastiani had been engaged lovers when copper was unexpectedly discovered on the Montebellan land marked out as her dowry, and to suggest that the Sebastianis had been so greedy as to murder the prince in order to prevent the marriage and retain the rich dowry land was an appalling slur against the Sebastiani name.

"In their view," she interrupted in a hot, unstoppable flood, "the Kamals figured if they made an accusation of foul play they could still get their hands on Delia's dowry land after Omar's and Delia's deaths. It was cynical manipulation then and it's cynical manipulation now. The Sebastianis were just as horrified as the Kamals when Omar was killed. Your family doesn't seem to want to remember that Delia was so unhappy over Omar's death she committed suicide! The Sebastianis were hit just as hard as the Kamals. And then to be accused of murder on top of it! The accusation was disgusting enough a hundred years ago. For your father to—"

Rashid held up a hand. "Whatever my father feels about this feud, Julia, I am not interested in prolonging it."

She stared at him, her anger arrested in surprise. This was the first she had ever heard that Rashid did not share his family's century-old obsession.

"Really? Why?"

"Because it is futile. It serves no good purpose. You must see this. If I could uncover the truth about Omar's death and satisfy my father's need to know, I would. But for myself I have no need to know. We are where we are. If Omar had lived, I would be only a very distant cousin of the Crown Prince of Tamir, if I existed at all. He did not live. I am Crown Prince. *Mash'Allah.* What occupies me is not how I came to this position, but how I will fulfill it for the people's good."

Julia said nothing.

"You and I could work together in this, Julia. And bequeath to our son a nation that lives in peace."

"Oh!" She drew a long, enlightened breath. So this was the answer. Not an elaborate game, not that he loved her, or even that he felt obliged to protect her unborn child.

It was a political marriage that motivated him. Her heart clenched painfully. She couldn't speak.

"Over the past few months I have had time to think," Rashid began quietly. "I thought about whether you had a reason for what happened. Sometimes I wondered if it was your intention to put us in this very situation—you pregnant with my child. I thought perhaps we had a similar view of the stupidity of this feud between our families, and how to heal it. Was I right?"

She stared at him. "What do you mean? That I planned to—that I meant to trick you into getting me pregnant so you'd be forced to marry me, for the sake of…" She faded off, swallowed, and continued in a whisper, "For the sake of peace between Tamir and Montebello?"

"Is it not so?"

She flung herself to her feet, unable to contain her feelings. "Is that what my child means to you—he'll force us into a political marriage that will be advantageous to your country?"

He was watching her from where he sat, not quite understanding her ferocity. "To both our countries, I hope," he said. "It is an end I have had in mind for a long time."

"An end you've had in mind for a long time?" she repeated blankly.

"It is years since I first thought of it as the surest way to re-establish peace between our countries. A marriage between the two ruling houses would be as advantageous now as it would have been a century ago. But when you married, I naturally gave up on it."

She blinked at him in amazement. "Why? You clearly didn't care about me personally."

"I did not know you personally. But I had seen you—"

She didn't want to hear the calm appraisal he had made of her suitability for the post of royal wife taken to cement a peace.

"Why not Christina, then? She wasn't married up until last month! Or Anna? She's available!"

"I never considered them," Rashid returned. Having said it, he was aware that such a position required some explanation. "Christina had renounced public life."

He understood only distantly that this was an after-the-fact rationalization. The truth was, he had never once considered Princess Christina in his plans—not even to reject her. And facing that fact now, he found it oddly inexplicable. He had given up his ideas of a political marriage with the Sebastianis when Julia married. "And Anna is too young."

"So when Luigi and I divorced your plans kicked right back in," she said dryly.

"It was not as simple as this, Julia. Let's not argue over the past. We have a child to think of. And our countries."

"There's a little drawback here. I'm not interested."

Rashid suddenly found himself exasperated. "Do you tell me you *prefer* to give birth to a child unmarried? You are a princess! You are in the public eye whatever you do! Have you not had enough of scandal?"

Julia gritted her teeth. The fact that he was only saying aloud what she had been saying to herself did nothing to calm her.

"I've already been through the worst of it in your absence," she said. "You may be a hero to your citizens, but don't try riding into *my* life on your white horse! You have overwhelmed me once. That will have to be enough for you. I intend to use my own judgement here, and that tells me—''

His lips tightened and his eyes narrowed as he watched her. ''What did you tell your father about how your pregnancy happened?'' he interrupted roughly.

''Not much.''

''And the police?''

''What are you talking about?''

''Have I been looking in the wrong direction? Is this merely another Sebastiani attempt to make the Kamals look like wild animals?''

Julia gasped. ''How dare you?''

''What have you told the world about how you got pregnant? Has our moment of madness become a rape, perhaps? Did I meet you at Harry and Mariel's wedding only to assault you?''

She gritted her teeth against overwhelming fury. ''I told them nothing beyond the bare facts.''

''How blind I've been! Of course you can't marry me, if you have been painting me in such colours! No wonder you are so furious! If this was a calculated move to make me look like a monster—of course a proposal of marriage is the last thing you want!''

A cold calm suffused Julia at his words. ''So because I won't marry you, you suddenly see a plot to blacken your reputation? Is it really impossible to believe that a woman could actually prefer life as a single mother to marriage with you? What an ego!''

''When there is so much good to be derived from the marriage—'' he began.

''Rashid,'' she said hoarsely, holding up a hand. ''I am not going to marry you. I have had one loveless marriage already. Believe me, it was one too many.''

"Loveless?" He reached out to cup her shoulder with one strong palm, stopping her retreat. "Why should it be loveless? We already know, Julia, how well we suit each other physically." His other hand gently tipped her chin up, then slipped around her back, drawing her irresistibly into his embrace.

Julia licked her lips. It was impossible to resist him when he touched her. Half of her longed to throw herself into his arms and accept the protection he offered.

But he was a Kamal. A member of the family that had blackened the proud Sebastiani name a century ago and was still raking over the coals of that ancient dispute.

Her eyes were suddenly burning. Julia twisted out of his embrace and stood facing him.

"It would be loveless," she said, with a precision born out of her determination not to weaken, "because you do not love me. And I do not love you."

Chapter 3

"Who the hell is this?" growled a deep male voice. Julia took a breath.

"Jack? This is Julia, Christina's sister. Is she there?"

"Julia." He cleared his throat. "Right. Hi. Hang on."

She heard the click of a lamp, and a confused murmur, then Christina's sleepy voice came on the line. "Tiss? What's up?"

"Oh, God, Squidge, you were sleeping! I'm sorry! I completely forgot the time difference. Is it really late?"

"No, that's okay," her sister said softly. "Actually…it's almost morning."

Julia gave a half laugh. "Oh, I'm sorry! I'll call back!"

"No, no, I'm awake now. Let me just…" Another murmur, followed by the noise of the receiver being set down on a hard surface, then her brother-in-law's voice in the distance.

"Going somewhere?"

"I'll talk in the other room so you can get back to sleep. Will you hang this up?"

"Yes. Where exactly are you taking the duvet?"

"To the other room. It's a bit chilly."

"Yes, it is. Bathrobe," she heard in tones of firm masculine command. "The duvet stays with me."

"My he-man! I thought you were immune to cold!" Christina's voice teased.

"The duvet is my insurance," he said. There was a smile in his voice. "You might forget where you were if you didn't have a warm bed to come back to."

"Oh, for sure!" There was a giggle from Christina that reminded Julia of those long-ago, carefree days of childhood. It was full of mischief and fun that was very unlike the cool Dr. Sebastiani Christina had become, and she thought, *They really are in love.*

Suddenly she felt like crying. *Why couldn't it happen like that for me? Why is it I only get proposed to for political convenience?*

"Are you still there, Tiss?"

There was the sound of the other receiver being gently replaced. Julia swallowed the lump in her throat. "Yeah, I'm here."

"What is it? Is everything all right?"

Where to begin?

"We heard about your engagement on the news. Congratulations." There was just a hint of hurt in her sister's voice. "It was a bit unexpected. First they were hinting that Rashid would deny pat—"

"Squidge, it was a surprise to me, too. The first I heard I was marrying him was when I read it in the *Messenger.*"

There was an sharp intake of breath, and she had the satisfaction of knowing she'd shocked Christina. "Excuse me?"

"He didn't bother to propose to me. He was so sure I'd be grateful for his offer he—"

"*Grateful!*" Christina yelped. "That's ridiculous."

"Thank you for that. I've been wondering if I'm the crazy one and should be panting with gratitude for being offered another chance at the married state."

"Is that his attitude? I thought at least that he loved you. I wasn't sure about your feelings, but—"

"He does not love me," Julia said ruthlessly.

"Then why would he want to marry you?"

"For the same reason he cooperated with NATO to get those terrorists. Because he wants to signal that Tamir's ready for an alliance with the West. He wants peace between us and Tamir. All those good things. And all we have to do is sacrifice our personal happiness for the good of our countries."

"My God." A long silence. "I'm sorry, Julia. The newscaster said…I confess I was really hoping that you did love him. It would be so nice to think of you being happy at last."

"No, it's the same old question here. Do I marry for the sake of the kingdom?"

"That's awful. What does Papa say about it?"

"They're still away, thank God. After an initial apoplectic attack, Papa backed off. I think he just can't cope. You know how old-fashioned he is, he hates to think of a baby being born outside of marriage. On the other hand…"

Christina gave a breathless little laugh. "On the other hand, when the father's a Kamal… Oh, Tiss, what a mess. What are you going to do?"

Suddenly the tears were threatening again. "That's what I called to ask you. What am I going to do? Got any ideas?"

A humming silence. Then, "It's not like they teach this

sort of thing in grad school, Tiss. Of course it would be better if you could be married, but not... Are you sure Rashid doesn't love you? Not even just enough to build on?''

''Yes, I'm sure. He told me himself he wanted the marriage for political purposes. Apparently he's had this dream of ending the feud through a marriage for years. He even imagined I might have deliberately got pregnant because I had the same goal, can you believe it?''

''No,'' Christina said. ''I can't believe anyone would think you're that calculating. But Julia, how *did* it happen?''

''I guess for a critical moment I went out of my mind. It's not based on anything real.''

''But you did—Tiss, forgive me if I'm missing something here, but there must be *something* between you.''

''Squidge,'' Julia began a bit desperately, ''it happened the night they announced they were calling off the search for Lucas. It was—I mean, my feelings were just so close to the surface.... I'm sure you must have felt the same.''

A long, sorrowing silence fell between the sisters. ''Has there been any news at all?'' Christina asked quietly.

''Nothing. And Papa still can't accept it. Well, neither can I, in my heart.''

''Me neither. And that's what caused you to lose your head with Rashid that night? Don't you think that just the very fact that you could turn to Rashid in such a moment shows—''

''No!'' Julia's heart was beating fast suddenly. ''I wasn't really attracted. I was just out of my mind.'' She said it like a mantra, as if the denial might protect her from something. Something like truth.

Christina sighed with regret. ''Well, you can't marry him, then. And you shouldn't feel you have to. This isn't the fourteenth century, Julia. Our countries don't need a marriage contract. They need a peace treaty."

Julia breathed deep. "Yes, you're right. You're right."

"Don't marry someone you don't love, Tiss. You know how bad a loveless marriage is, but you don't know how good a loving one is. You deserve better next time around—a man you love, and who loves you, with a once-in-a-lifetime sort of love."

Warmth and certainty flowed through the phone line. She could hear the smile behind Christina's words that said her sister had found that kind of love. She felt a pang so painful she almost gasped.

"All right. Thanks, Squidge. Go back to bed now," she ordered softly.

"Well...are you really all right?"

"Yes."

"Good night, then."

"Night. Give my love to Jack."

"Mmmmm." It was a sound of rich happiness. "And Tiss—"

"Yes?"

"Don't let them make you do anything you don't want to do."

Julia sat with her hand on the phone for a long time after they had hung up, feeling the connection with her sister. Imagining Christina going back into the bedroom and snuggling down beside her husband, knowing he loved her.... How lucky they were. Alone together on their honeymoon in the middle of nowhere, no staff, no bodyguards, no servants. Just two people who loved each other.

You don't know how good a loving marriage is.

Suddenly the tears burned up and overflowed, and this time she couldn't stop them. It was as if she was crying for everything at once—for Lucas, for her loveless marriage, for her child who would be raised without a father…for the fact that Rashid wanted to marry her for all the wrong reasons.

A newsmagazine with his photo on the cover was lying on her bedside table. No doubt because some romantic member of the domestic staff imagined she would want the picture of her intended. She glanced down at his face. His eyes were at once stern and laughing, and they seemed to pierce her defences.

If he had pretended he loved me instead of telling me the truth, I might have imagined…. She quickly broke off the train of thought. *Thank God he didn't. My emotions are close to the surface, and I miss Lucas so much. I'll have to be careful. I could weaken. I weakened once before.*

At the age of nineteen, Princess Julia had felt herself to be at the doorway of an exciting future. She had passed her university entrance exams with excellent marks at the Swiss school she attended, and a small documentary film she had made as an extracurricular project, about Montebello's famous street market, had won her a place at a prestigious college of film in London. That was the future she had yearned for. She had wanted to make films.

Papa had had other ideas. His ideas all centred upon duty. And he wanted Julia to come home, marry and have children in the good, old-fashioned Montebellan tradition.

He even had a husband all picked out for her. Handsome Luigi di Vitale Ferrelli, scion of one of Montebello's wealthiest aristocratic families, was among Julia's large circle of friends. Papa knew that Julia already liked Luigi. The di Vitale Ferrellis had always been staunch allies of the Sebastianis, but never before had there been a marriage to cement the bond.

Julia and Luigi had announced their engagement and the

country had gone crazy with delight. She was so beautiful, he was so handsome—and one of Montebello's own! So much better than marrying her off to some foreign prince.

The engagement would be a long one. Luigi, only two years older than Julia, was learning about his family's business from the ground up. He was often out of the country, travelling to distant parts of the family empire, and his schedule was impossible to predict.

Julia's father would not agree to her going to London, even so. Instead she stayed in the palace, working with her father, learning a job she enjoyed, but would never be called upon to perform.

Julia had believed—or wanted to believe—that the liking between her and Luigi could develop into love. Lots of the girls in her set were half in love with him. He was good fun, and had charm.

Luigi was very respectful, and surprisingly old-fashioned. Right from the start he treated her as untouchable. "Don't worry, Julia," he assured her during one of their brief meetings between his flying trips. "I won't rush you. There's plenty of time. When we get married, everything will fall into place."

For a while she accepted it. But there was a lot of pairing off among her friends, and Julia began to yearn for romance in her own life. Once, when Luigi came home on one of his increasingly rare visits, she tried to hint this fact to him.

He took her in his arms and kissed her passionately for the first time. His passion seemed almost anguished, and Julia had responded openly, wrapping her arms around his neck and pressing into his embrace.

Then he had stopped. "No, Julia," he said. "We can wait. We should wait. Be patient. My father will bring me home soon to work at head office, and we can be married."

The months passed, and stretched into the first year, and

then the second, and Luigi never budged from this position. He swore that he loved her, with a torment in his eyes that mystified her. If they loved each other and they were going to marry, what was the point of his torment? She teased him, she touched him, she enticed him, using all the confidence of her new young sexuality, trying to break down the wall of his reserve.

Her attempts failed. And gradually, humiliatingly, she saw the truth—much as he liked her, and she didn't doubt that, Luigi just didn't *want* to make love to her. When she finally accepted it, she was awash with embarrassment and shame for the way she had exposed herself.

And she had a clear understanding that marriage between them could never work. She made the decision to go to her father and tell him that she wanted out of the engagement.

With cruel precision of timing, before she could act on her decision, her sister Christina's scandal broke. Her photo appeared in the tabloids—topless, with the newspapers making no secret of the fact that it was her own boyfriend who had sold them the pictures.

Before she could talk to her father, King Marcus came to speak to her. To protect Christina from further media attention, he wanted to make the date of Julia's wedding firm. He had spoken to Luigi's father, who had agreed that it was time to bring the young man home and let him settle down. The wedding would be next month.

Julia had tried to tell her father then, but it was too late. It was the first time her father had pleaded with her. "Please don't bring another scandal on our heads, Julia. I ask this as your father and as the king. Montebello asks you...."

The wedding had thrilled her father's subjects, but Julia had repeated her vows with misery in her heart. And in

Luigi's eyes had been a hunted look that told her, too late, how desperately he, too, had wanted out.

She was not surprised at his complete inability to consummate the marriage. She was a lot less naive at twenty-two than she had been at nineteen. She tried to help in every way she could, but the end was always the same—frustration and anger.

After a while Luigi began to blame her, and worse, to mock her attempts to arouse him. That was the beginning of a much deeper humiliation. Luigi told her she was the only woman with whom he was impotent, listed the names of others—her friends, sometimes—with whom he had had very successful, satisfactory flings. Every time he bedded another woman he would brag to her about it.

She learned to doubt his bragging, just as she learned to dread the appearance of the regular stories in the press speculating about the reasons for the golden couple's lack of children. Inevitably it would mean Luigi coming to her bedroom to try again. And blaming her.

She knew that he was telling his friends that she was frigid and that was the reason for the lack of children. His friends dutifully leaked the information to journalists. When she pointed out the unfairness of this, he responded with a furious attack on her lack of femininity, lack of sex appeal…*what do you want me to tell them? The truth? That you disgust me?*

Julia buried her misery in work. She was intelligent, and she had an instinct for public work. Her father came to rely on her more and more for a calm and reasoned opinion on foreign and domestic affairs.

Publicly, and within the family, she and Luigi presented a united front. No one knew how deeply, fundamentally flawed the storybook marriage was.

Until the scandal broke like a tidal wave over all their

heads. Without warning, photographs of Luigi in an unmistakably compromising position with George Dimarno, Julia's own chauffeur, were published in a tabloid paper.

Even the fact that the media universally condemned Luigi and sympathized with Julia was unbearable. They speculated endlessly about his treatment of her. They published tidbits from palace staff eager to set the record straight at last. In the end they published the horrible, self-exculpating interview that Luigi, driven almost to insanity, had given. It was awful to see him expose himself so brutally, painful to read how he had turned on her.

That interview had been the breaking point for Julia. She withdrew into herself, distancing herself from public life, and even from her family, as she slowly sank into the depression she had been keeping at bay for so long.

It was himself Luigi hated, not her. She could see now that he had rejected his own sexuality, rejected for as long as he could, even the knowledge of it. She could understand, but understanding did not undo the cruel damage he had inflicted on her sense of herself.

It took her a year to get through it. A long, cold year in which she had had no interest in life, no appetite. The only place she felt comfortable was alone in her private gym. She ate too little, exercised too much, lost too much weight. She had enjoyed the feeling of control over her body. It was the only part of her life over which she felt any control.

And then one day the long black tunnel showed light, and Julia realized that there would be an end to her shapeless, colourless days. She resolved to start over, to make a life for herself more in line with what she wanted.

But it wasn't a light at the end of the tunnel. It was Rashid Kamal, on a collision course.

Chapter 4

"The course of true love not running quite smoothly?" Nadia asked Rashid over dinner that night. Brother and sister were alone in the palace in Tamir. Everyone else was at one or another function tonight, except for their brother Hassan, who was miles away in the oil fields as usual. They were sitting at a little table on the East Terrace, overlooking the gorge. In the velvety darkness the sea rushed and shushed against the rocks.

Rashid leaned back in his chair. "Why do you say so?" he hedged. They were speaking English so that the serving staff would not understand.

His sister smiled mockingly. "Because Nargis told me. And before you ask, Nargis looks after my wardrobe. The staff is buzzing with the news that you are being uncharacteristically rude and withdrawn today. Everyone knows you went to Montebello to talk to Julia earlier."

"Do they? Damn it!"

"So there's speculation about whether it's because Princess Julia has accepted you, in which case you're regretting the loss of your playboy lifestyle, or rejected you, in which case your heart is broken. Naturally everyone prefers to believe the intensely romantic version. Care to comment?''

"Damn it to hell."

"*I* believe it's nothing more than a bad headache," Nadia said with a grin, "but then I'm your sister and I know it's a rare woman who makes you snarly."

"She *is* a rare woman," he couldn't stop himself saying, and watched Nadia's eyebrows go up.

"Ah! And am I to infer from this that she has rejected your proposal?"

He was aware of mounting irritation. "Yes, she has! I can't figure her out!" He glared at his sister as if she were part of this mystery. "Why would she turn me down? She's pregnant and the press have been on her like wolves! Why won't she see that—"

He stopped because Nadia was laughing. "Haven't you ever before met with a woman who turned you down, Rashid?"

"I've never proposed to a woman before," he said shortly.

"You didn't propose to Julia, the way I hear it."

"What do you mean? I proposed very publicly!"

Nadia shook her head. "There's a difference, big brother, between asking a woman to marry you and telling the world that she's going to marry you and then expecting her to agree."

He looked at her, indignant. "You're the one who advised me to rush my fences."

"With *Father,* not with Julia! Can't you see how arrogant it is to assume that a woman will jump at the chance to marry you? And a beautiful princess, too! Why on earth didn't you talk to Julia first?"

"You know what the speculation was like! What was so wrong? I realized what Julia had been going through for the past few months and wanted to put an end to it."

"Knight in shining armour, huh?"

Rashid moved his shoulders, reminded of Julia's *Don't try riding into my life on your white horse.* "Look," he said forcefully, as if somehow he were justifying himself to Julia, "if I delayed, someone was going to put words in my mouth! I didn't want Julia reading that I was surprised to hear I'd been named the father of her child, or considering my options, or something like that. What would be worse, do you think? To get a proposal after someone has spent time considering whether he's really the father of your child, or—"

"Pax!" His sister lifted her hands and laughed. "This is Nadia here, not Julia, notice?"

He subsided with a clenched jaw.

"I couldn't make her see it."

"A new experience, I take it. I think I'm going to like Julia. When I remember all the women who have cried on my shoulder trying to solve the mystery of how to reach your feelings, it does my heart good."

Rashid frowned. "This has nothing to do with my feelings. I'm trying to do what's right for all concerned!"

"Noble. Sure about that?"

"Of course I'm sure. What do you mean?"

"Well, there is a certain question of how she got pregnant in the first place."

Rashid grunted. "It was nothing but a kind of—insanity."

"At your age," Nadia agreed in cheerful incredulity. "I see."

"And however it happened, it's done. What I have to think about now is what I'm going to do in the future. Julia

is going to issue a statement denying the engagement tomorrow, I think.'' Rashid irritably waved away the waiter
who was trying to pour him more coffee. ''I've got to prevent that.''

Nadia opened her eyes at him in mute reproach and,
pointedly gracious, said to the waiter in Arabic, ''Yes,
thank you, Iqbal, I will have some more coffee.

''And how are you going to do that?'' she asked, when
Iqbal had retreated.

''I have to swear you to secrecy, Nadia.''

''All right.''

''I've got to get her alone. I think she'd see sense if she
didn't have that coterie of Kamal-haters around her.''

Nadia's eyebrows went up. ''And?''

Rashid rubbed his chin and stared out into the darkness.
For a moment they listened to the sound of the waterfall.

''I'm going to have to kidnap her.''

It was when Lucas's plane went missing, oddly, that Julia
woke up at last. Perhaps because she suddenly saw how
precious life was. And she had given away a whole year
of hers.

No one knew whether Lucas would be found alive or
dead. All they had was hope. Julia had returned to the family emotionally to share that hope with her sisters and her
parents, and keep it alive.

She had learned a lot during her year of self-exile. She
felt she had come a long, long distance from the repressed,
self-doubting perfectionist she had become in order to cope
with Luigi's rejection.

Mariel de Vouvray had been her friend since the two
girls had attended private school in Switzerland together.
When Mariel's wedding invitation had arrived, she had

turned it down, like every other invitation she received during that year of darkness.

But as the day grew closer, Julia began to change her mind. She and Mariel had been very close for a while, and it was only physical distance that had changed that. She wanted to see Mariel married to her prince. Haroun al Jawadi was a man Julia didn't know, brother of the new Sultan of Bagestan.

Mariel had said on her invitation that the wedding was going to be "as private and personal as we can make it. We emphatically are *not* selling the story to *Hello!* magazine. So you won't be on show—we hope!—if you come."

She knew that a last-minute acceptance would cause logistical problems. The high-profile wedding guests were staying overnight in the château where the wedding was being held, as Julia had been invited to do. She didn't want to put Mariel to the trouble of a reshuffle. She also knew that if word got out that Princess Julia was making her first public appearance at the wedding after a year's exile it would boot up the media interest in the wedding.

She decided to go incognito. She travelled on her private passport and put up in a tiny family hotel where, if she was recognized, at least no one made a fuss.

The ceremony itself would take place in the beautiful old chapel attached to the château. Julia slipped into the church with a group of non-celebrity arrivals. No photographer recognized her in the ankle-length dark blue coat and low-brimmed hat. For good measure she had pulled her white silk scarf up over her chin.

Inside, she sat on the bride's side of the church, tucking herself beside a pillar where she couldn't be seen from most of the church. She couldn't see, either, and she didn't look around for people she knew.

So she didn't realize until the ceremony was almost over that one of the guests was Rashid Kamal.

"We need to talk," Rashid's voice said firmly in her ear. Julia twitched nervously, feeling hunted. She shifted the receiver to her other hand.

"Do we? Why?" She had had a mostly sleepless night last night, and she wasn't ready for this.

She could almost hear him gritting his teeth. "Because you are pregnant with my child and I want to marry you. And we need a reasoned discussion of the choices before you go public with a denial of our engagement."

Julia was silent.

"You haven't already done it, have you?"

"No." Coward that she was. She should have picked up the phone when the mood was on her and called the newspaper reporter most loyal to her. She had told herself that she needed breathing space before stirring up yet another round of speculation. "Not yet."

"No, of course not," he reminded himself. "Someone would have called me for a comment immediately if you had."

"And what would you have said?" She did not want a war with Rashid to be fought in the media. But she did not forget that he was the one who had put her in this position.

"What could I say? That I regretted your decision. And I do, Julia. But I don't believe that decision is final, or should be."

"It is!" she cried, almost panicking. "Totally final! I'm going to do it today!"

Damn it, did he *always* have to handle her wrong?

"Look," he said, as calmly as he could. "I'd like us to talk. Before you do that."

She sighed uneasily, not sure why she didn't feel safe

talking to him. He had such charisma. Suppose he convinced her to marry him against her better judgement? Once was enough.

"All right, go ahead," she said, suddenly wishing she had Christina here to support her through this.

She heard him expel an exasperated breath. "Not over the phone, damn it, Julia! I need to see you face-to-face. And away from the palace somewhere."

Panic threatened in her stomach. The baby did a somersault. "Where? We'll be chased wherever we go."

He said dryly, "I think I can promise to get us to a venue where there will be no journalists."

"I don't see what there is to talk about."

"How about the fact that at the moment a Sebastiani child is the only direct descendant of the Kamal ruling house in the next generation and my father's people will want to know whether he's to be in line for the throne?" Rashid said impatiently. "Do you feel that question could be important enough to discuss?"

The panic rushed up to grip her throat. Might the old man name her son a prince of Tamir? She supposed he had the right to confer the status of prince on his illegitimate grandson, if he wished. She was pretty sure that in the dim and distant past of Tamir, Rashid himself had a bloodline that dated back to a favourite concubine.

What kind of chaos would it cause in her life, to be raising the child destined, however briefly, for the throne of another nation? An enemy nation. And what suffering was in store when Rashid married and had a legitimate son, as he surely would, and her son was displaced as heir?

"He can't do that!" she cried. Rashid was right. They had to talk. "All right, what do you want me to do?"

"I want you to agree not to issue any statement until we've talked."

Her nerves tightened. "Twenty-four hours," she said.

She heard him breathe. "That's not much time."

"Twenty-four hours," she repeated.

"Twenty-four hours it is. If you can convince your father not to have my helicopter shot down on arrival," Rashid said with mordant humour, "I'll pick you up in an hour. Pack a swimsuit."

It was a beautiful ceremony. Mariel was stunning, with an unusual and artistic scrunch of white veil and flowers framing her head, and a gorgeous silk brocade dress styled with a medieval flavour that exactly suited the chapel. Haroun al Jawadi looked proud and handsome, and every time he gazed down at his bride a shiver of delight went through the congregation.

She wasn't sure how Rashid Kamal had drawn her eye. When the congregation was kneeling, Julia was no longer hidden by her pillar. A baby started to babble, and her gaze automatically flicked towards the groom's side of the church.

A man's black hair was burnished by the winter sunlight streaming in through a stained-glass window. She watched with a smile of absent pleasure before she suddenly recognized the shape of his brow and chin.

Then she pressed her lips together and resolutely bowed her head, feeling as if someone had just walked over her grave. It wasn't the first time they'd been at the same function, but always before it had been at large, formal gatherings. She'd never been invited to such an intimate gathering with him before. There probably weren't a hundred people here.

She had no one to blame but herself. If she had accepted the invitation in the normal way, of course Mariel would have forewarned her. And if she had thought for even a moment, she might have guessed that the Crown Prince of Tamir might number among the friends of the groom. For a few moments Julia considered slipping away immediately after the ceremony, but she didn't want to go without even saying hello.

"Julia! Oh, thank you for coming after all! How wonderful to see you!" Mariel cried with delighted surprise when, in the château later, Julia came over to give her friend a hug. "I'm so glad! It must mean you're feeling better."

Then her eyes widened at a thought. "Oh, my goodness!" she said faintly.

Julia laughed. "It's all right, I've seen him."

"He's one of Harry's best friends," Mariel confided in a low voice. "I was going to warn you if you accepted."

"I'm keeping out of his way. We've done this kind of thing before, after all."

"Maybe he won't even recognize you! You look so different, Julia! Have you changed your style completely?"

"Do you like it?"

"Absolutely! You look—softer. You're way too thin, but—there's a glow that wasn't there before. And I love your hair! Is it metaphorical? Are you letting your hair down at last?"

Julia enjoyed herself at the party that followed, and it was easy to avoid Rashid Kamal. People recognized her, but there were quite a few celebrity and royal faces in the room. No stranger paid her particular attention until a gorgeous redhead she vaguely recognized stopped beside her.

"I was just wondering if you'd heard any more news," she said apologetically, when the two women had exchanged greetings. Astrid had dated Lucas for a while a couple of years ago.

"There's nothing," Julia said sadly. "We're just waiting."

"But it was definitely his plane?"

Julia frowned. "What do you mean?"

"The piece of wreckage they found yesterday. Are they definite that—" Astrid broke off in horror when she saw Julia's face. "My God, haven't you heard?"

Julia clutched at her. "They—they found the wreckage? Lucas? Did they find—" she gasped breathlessly.

"Oh, hell! I'm so sorry to be the one to tell you! But I don't—the newscast I heard just said a piece of wreckage had been found and they thought—"

Julia was already groping in her bag for her phone. "I left home yesterday." And last night had been spent in the tiny, old-fashioned hotel with no TV in the room. Her mother had said nothing last night when she phoned. "Excuse me, I've got to go and phone!"

She dashed out the nearest door, into a hallway. But there were people strolling up and down, and she took the nearest stairwell up. She came out in a shadowed, darkly wainscotted hall, with doors along one side and arched windows on the other. Looking for a place to hide, Julia ran to a corner at the far end that was partly protected by a carved panel, and huddled in the darkness, dialing home.

It was the private line, and her mother answered. "Mama? It's Julia!" she breathed.

"Hello, darling. Having a good time? Where are you?"

"At the château. Mama, someone just told me—"

"Oh, Julia," said her mother, and those words were enough. Her hopes that it could be a mistake died. She sobbed a breath.

"It's true, then?"

"Yes, we heard late last night." Her mother's voice held the memory of tears. "After you called. I didn't—I didn't want you to be alone with the news, so I didn't call back. I suppose it was foolish to hope you wouldn't hear before you got home. I'm sorry, darling. I wanted you to have a good time at your friend's wedding. You've had so little enjoyment lately."

"I don't know any details, Mama. Just that they've..." She swallowed, her throat aching with unshed tears. "Is it true they've found the plane?" Julia asked.

Her mother's voice trembled. "A piece of the wreckage. They're pretty sure—" she swallowed and continued in a calmer voice "—pretty sure it's Lucas's plane."

"Was there any sign of—of Lucas?"

"No. At the moment they seem to think the plane broke up in the air. Julia, the worst of it is, they—the authorities there have called off the air search."

It was like hearing her own death warrant.

"No!" she protested, and the unshed tears burst from her in a flood. "Noooo! Oh, *Lucas!"*

"Anna's very distressed. Your father is insisting that some sort of search should continue, but—well, at this distance it's hard to know exactly what's...what's...oh, Julia," she wailed helplessly. "What are we going to do?"

"Going off with Rashid Kamal?" her father repeated, his voice rough with incredulity. "Why? Where?"

Anna was staring at her sister with a wild surmise. Only the queen went on calmly drinking her coffee.

Julia bit her lip. She might have known she'd run into flak on this. It wasn't anything she liked, either, but it had to be done. She wished her father would accept it without a lot of argument. Argument just made her more jittery.

"I am not *going off* with him, Papa. We are simply going somewhere we can talk for a few hours over lunch."

"Where?" he repeated grimly.

"I don't know. Somewhere we can be reasonably alone, I imagine. I've left it to him."

"You've lost your bearings, Julia!" He looked at his wife for support.

They were sitting in the small breakfast room over a late Saturday breakfast. Anna was now hiding a smile. She flicked Julia a conspiratorial, admiring look and picked up her cup. Julia wanted to cry, *I am not sneaking off to a lovers' assignation!*

The queen remained silent, and her father returned to the attack. "I forbid you to go anywhere with a Kamal! Have you forgotten your brother's fate?"

"Papa, you have surely accepted by now that it wasn't the Kamals who did that. If anyone, it was the Brothers of Darkness. And who has done most lately to spike their guns?"

Her father subsided a little. "That still doesn't make it safe for you—"

"Look," Julia interrupted. "I don't like it any better than you do. But like it or not, Rashid Kamal is the father of my child. And at the moment, according to him, his father is contemplating naming my son as his heir. Whether that's an empty threat or not, it just points up the fact that there are things we have to discuss. And since I don't want those things leaked to the media, we are going somewhere alone, and I will not be taking a bodyguard."

She won the argument. But by the end she was so worn out with pretending to trust Rashid Kamal that she was sweating with nerves.

The helicopter beat the air as it slowly settled onto the grass, whipping Julia's long hair and the full skirt of her soft yellow dress. She put a hand up to hold her hat. Rashid watched the way her dress clung to her stomach, looking for the signs that a child was growing there.

When he cut the rotor, she came across the lawn towards him and leaned in the passenger door, peering towards the seats in the back of the helicopter. Rashid pulled his mouthpiece away from his chin so she could recognize him.

"Hello!" he cried over the engine noise.

Julia did a double take. She hadn't been expecting him to be piloting the helicopter himself, and a fresh wave of nervous energy swept her.

"Hello!" Her voice held the sound of her determination to keep this pleasant. She had a deep, primitive urge to turn and flee.

"Can you climb in?" He spoke so matter-of-factly that her fears were momentarily calmed. *He's a Kamal,* she told herself. *That doesn't mean he's going to murder me in cold blood.*

He leaned across to offer her a hand, but she clambered in without his help. He frowned to himself without knowing why. Something to do with wanting to be needed. Especially because she was pregnant.

With his son.

He helped her strap herself in, however, and gestured towards a headset in front of her. Julia took off her straw hat and slipped the headset over her ears. A moment later the chopper lifted smoothly off under his guidance, and they were airborne.

"Did you bring a bathing suit?" Rashid's voice said in her headset.

It felt too intimate to have his voice inside her head like this. It reminded her of the last time she had heard him so close. Then he had not needed the assistance of a headset to give the impression of closeness; his voice had sounded close because his mouth was against her hair.

Beautiful, he had murmured. *You are so beautiful….*

Julia's cheeks burned with the memory. "I did," she said, hefting her drawstring bag as evidence without meeting his eyes. She dropped the bag between her feet and turned to look out. He had taken them out over the water and was heading north.

So the private place he had in mind was not on any of the Tamir Islands. She had wondered if he meant to take her to his horse farm on Siraj.

"Are we going to a yacht?" she wondered, half to herself, forgetting that her headset, too, had a microphone.

"No, an island."

"An island? Rashid, I don't have a passport with me!"

He laughed. "Stop worrying, Julia." Again his voice was intimate and seductive in her ears. "Your seat reclines. Lie back and relax."

In the cocoon of the helicopter with him, she felt strangely detached from the normal world. If she had not known Rashid was a Kamal, she would have felt an instinctive trust of him.

There was nothing she could do about this situation except start screaming to be taken home. Or go along with it.

She was tired after her sleepless night, and she would do better in the coming discussion if she caught some sleep now. With a resigned shrug, Julia found the mechanism, reclined her seat, and, with the sun bright above them, and sparkling almost painfully from the deep blue of the Mediterranean below, closed her eyes and let herself drowse. The memory was never far away….

Chapter 5

After her mother hung up, she had crouched on the floor, her head in her arms, alternately sobbing her brother's name and begging God to let him live. "Lucas, oh, Lucas! Please, God, please, no!"

She'd thought she'd faced the possibility, been prepared for the worst ever since learning that Lucas's plane had gone missing. She saw now what an illusion that was. Now, when all her hopes came crashing down around her, she could see how wildly she had been hoping, how she had staved off any real acceptance that the worst might happen.

She was crouched in the gloom, sobbing wildly, when a hand touched her shoulder.

"Please go away," she hiccuped desperately, hiding her face in her hands. "Please."

"I can't do that," said a voice. "I can't leave you here like this. Come." The voice was strong with masculine authority, and perhaps it was because she felt lost without

Lucas in the world, felt as if her sheet anchor was gone, that she took comfort from his presence.

He drew her to her feet, and she allowed him to do it, then buried her face in a strong, comforting shoulder as he held her and gently stroked her hair. "My brother," she sobbed. "My brother—"

She was swept by another bout of inconsolable weeping, and her knees collapsed. He caught her as she slumped, and without a word bent and swung her up in his arms.

His hold was strong and sure, like her father's when she was a child. He strode down the corridor and stopped by a door, and she heard the sound of a key in the lock. In another moment she was inside in deep darkness. He bent and she felt something soft under her back. A bed. He tried to straighten, but she clung to him. "Hold me," she begged. "Just hold me for a minute, please."

She heard his indrawn breath, felt him stiffen and then relax. Then he sat on the bed and leaned down over her. His arm slipped under her back, a hand stroked her hair, and she felt comforted.

"I love him so much," she explained. "So much. All my life he's been..." But words couldn't describe her bond with Lucas.

"Tell me," he said.

There was a *whuff! whuff!* of tissues coming out of the box, and his hand pressed them into hers. His voice and his being were unfamiliar. She felt a sudden sense of liberation. He was a stranger. She didn't know him, he didn't know her. For once in her life she could be herself.

A part of her whispered that it was foolish, that as soon as the lights went on he *would* know her, but grief made her slightly drunk: she didn't care. She wiped her face and began to tell him about Lucas, how close they had always been, how much it increased her grief that during the past year she had cut herself off even from him…her guilt and woe all came out together.

"They've called off the search. Why have they done that?" she begged, as if he might really have the answer. "Lucas might be out there, hurt, wounded, and it's so cold in the mountains!"

She sobbed wildly. "I can't bear to think of him, cold, in pain—and the wild animals! Bears and lynxes…and wolves…do they have wolves there?" Somehow that seemed worse than anything else. That he might be savaged by wolves.

"I don't know," he said.

"He's my brother, my only brother!" she cried. "And he might be lying there waiting for someone to come, and now no one is even *looking* for him!"

Gradually her tears subsided, and she was simply there, on a strange bed, in a stranger's arms. He was holding her, and murmuring words of comfort.

She heaved a long, shuddering sigh, and suddenly she *was* comforted. Comforted, and something more. She sniffed, wiped her nose, and took a shuddering breath. "Thank you," she murmured, against his neck. "I think— I'm all right now."

His face turned to hers in the darkness. "Sure?" he whispered. The intimacy made her tremble. She swallowed and nodded mutely, her still tear-damp temple against his cheek. The world seemed to hold its breath. It was the most natural thing in the world when he lowered his head and his mouth sought hers.

She clung to him as a deep, honeyed pleasure fountained up in her, and parted her lips under the gentle demand of his mouth. Her arms slipped around his neck, and the world swooped away from under her. She was suddenly dizzy with pleasure and anticipation.

His arms tightened possessively around her, and his mouth became more demanding, more urgent. She thrilled to the masculine hunger she had never experienced before, and every expression of his desire took her own need a notch higher. Was this what it was like, then, when a man actually wanted you? How delicious! How thrilling to feel that you were desirable, to feel the arms around you tremble with something other than tormented self-disgust!

Then abruptly he lifted his mouth from hers, and she heard a hoarse breathing, as if he were struggling for calm.

"I'm sorry," he whispered. His hand came up to stroke her cheek.

"It's all right," she assured him.

"We have to stop."

She could hear the hunger still in his voice. "Why?" she cried softly. He shook his head and she felt him reach out a hand.

And then there was light. A small pool of warm, golden light that glowed and sparkled in her "lucky" bracelet. She wondered absently if it was an omen that that was the first thing she saw.

A lamp by an old-fashioned four-poster bed. In a room out of another century. There was the box of tissues under the lamp. Dark, strong hands picked up a water carafe that sat there, too, and neatly filled a glass. He turned to her. "Drink."

She reached for the glass, looking up with a grateful half smile through the mess of hair and tears that shrouded her vision. Then with a gasping shriek she shrank back.

"Oh, my *God!*" she cried.

"Your devil, I think," he contradicted ironically.

"Rash— You're Rashid Kamal!"

"I thought a little light on the subject might change your mind about things."

He continued to hold out the glass.

"Why...why...why did you—" she babbled.

"Because I wouldn't pass by even an animal suffering the way you were. Now drink this—it's not poisoned. Or do you want me to taste it first?" He did so, then held it out again.

She had a horrible headache suddenly, the result of too many tears. Her face was hot and sticky, her hair glued to her cheeks. Julia brushed the tangles aside, took the glass and obediently drank.

Rashid Kamal, meanwhile, stepped into the little attached bathroom. She heard water running. A moment later he was beside her, tilting up her chin with one hand as he wiped her face with a damp, cool cloth.

"Thank you." She was hiccuping with the aftermath of tears, and perhaps passion, her breath catching uncontrollably in her diaphragm. She tried to smile, her mouth trembling with the effort.

One dark strong eyebrow went up and down again. "I'll take the smile as read," he remarked in a level voice, got up and tossed the cloth back into the bathroom.

She couldn't think of anything to say.

There were two gothic-arched, mullioned windows in the ancient stone wall, behind which twilight was fading into night. The walls of the room were wainscotted up to a height of six feet. Above them the plaster was a pale cream.

The room was quite small, very cosy. There was space only for the big oak four-poster, a small desk and chair, and a wooden chest. In the window embrasures were set small seats padded with blue velvet to match the hangings on the bed.

Rashid Kamal leaned against one of the embrasures, watching her. Through the window behind his head, she could just make out the outlines of the roof of another wing of the château. Stars were coming out in a clear sky.

This part of the château must be fourteenth century, she guessed. There was comfort in the timelessness. The room had a warm, sweet atmosphere, and she felt a deep reluctance to leave it, in spite of who was with her. The charged mood of a moment ago still affected her.

He was watching her from dark, unreadable eyes.

Her father believed that it was the Kamals who had orchestrated Lucas's disappearance. He would be utterly shocked—traumatized—if he could see her here. But, much as she hated the Kamals, Julia had never accepted it. What did they stand to gain from Lucas's death? Revenge for a century-old murder? It didn't make sense in the modern world.

She felt torn in two suddenly.

"I guess I should get back to the party," she murmured. "My handbag…"

"It's here," he said, moving to the end of the bed, but she saw it in the same moment, lying by her feet, her mobile phone to one side. They reached for it together. Their hands touched. Her bracelet glinted in the shadows. She smelled his aftershave, as though a pulse of his blood had sent a burst of it into the room. He looked at her lips, and she instinctively licked them. He straightened, leaving her in possession of her bag.

"I'll just get cleaned up a little, if that's all right."

"Of course."

She stared at herself in the bathroom mirror as she washed her face, trying to make sense of what she was now feeling for Rashid Kamal. How could she be so wildly attracted to such a man? All her muscles seemed slowed with hunger. Was she just coming unhinged because of Lucas? Was it simple deprivation?

When she came out of the bathroom again, he was folding a shirt into a small case. Her heart was choking her. Rashid's gaze met hers. She felt stifled. The air was thick with unspoken desire.

"Thank you for—"

"This is my room," he said, his voice hard with self-control. "I'm leaving now. If you want to stay…"

Julia swallowed. She did not want to leave. She did not want him to go. But he was Rashid Kamal. "Thank you," she whispered, struggling with herself. "Uh, but—"

She was standing between him and the ancient mahogany chest, where his clothes were hanging. He reached his hands to her upper arms. Later, remembering this, she would cringe with shame, telling herself that his intention had been only to move her out of the way. But in the charged moment it seemed to her that he reached for her out of uncontrollable desire.

She cried his name, and sank against him, and whatever he had intended, this was his undoing. His arms wrapped around her, hard with possession, and his mouth came down to plunder her hungry, willing lips.

"We're here," Rashid's voice murmured in her ears. Julia awoke feeling refreshed, but with no idea how long she had been asleep. She looked out and saw that they were losing height on the approach to a small island, and smiled with surprised pleasure.

It was a long, narrow island, with beautiful white sand beaches in several rocky coves along its south coast, and spectacular rock cliffs rising behind. On the easternmost tip, in a small, protected bay, was a villa. There was a pine forest on the western side of the island, and a grove of fruit and olive trees nearer the house. Everywhere there were flowering shrubs.

She saw a terra-cotta-tiled terrace and roof half smothered with purple, red and pink blossoms amidst the lush green surrounding the house. And then they were down and settling onto an open area within the orchard, which obviously served as heliport.

"Goodness, where are we?" she cried. "What a beautiful place!"

The simplicity of it entranced her. There was no swimming pool, no tennis court, no architectural arrogance. A house had been built, long ago, apparently, and with the minimum of disturbance to the island's integrity. There were a couple of small sheds, but she had seen no sign of another building that might house guards or secret service personnel.

No fences.

She jumped out and stood for a moment listening to the sounds we call silence. The shush of the sea roiling up the clean white sand. The wind stirring the leaves and blossoms. The cry of birds. Nothing else.

She could almost have wept.

"Come," said Rashid. Slipping his arm lightly around her waist, he led her through the orange and olive and lemon trees and then between high banks of dark green shrubbery that were bursting with bloom, and onto the broad terrace at the front of the house which she had seen from the air.

Beneath her feet were worn terra-cotta tiles. Around her, a low wall of white painted stucco held back the twelve-foot-high ranks of bougainvillea, rose and rhododendron. Over their heads, an arching pergola that curved from one side of the terrace to the other against the house was tangled with vines, from which clusters of purple grapes entrancingly hung down. Behind the house and beyond, the tip of the island was rugged with a high protective sweep of tumbled rock that half encircled the tiny bay with its white sand beach sloping gently into the turquoise sea.

Julia heaved a huge sigh, as if a heavy cloak were slipping from her shoulders.

Rashid, watching her, saw the tension leave her like a physical thing, and only then really understood what pressures were on her. He wondered how many of them could be laid at his door. It couldn't have been pleasant, facing her father and telling him who the father of her child was.

She turned and smiled at him. "Who else is here?"

His look at her was slightly sombre, as if he were worried about her reaction to what he was going to say. "No one. We are alone on the island."

Julia laughed in startled delight. "Really and truly? Not one soul? No bodyguards anywhere? Not even a bartender?"

He grinned and shook his head.

No human voice save their own. No one to call her Your Royal Highness. Her trembling smile stretched from ear to ear, quirking up at the ends with a sweetness that lifted his own troubles from him.

"Where are we? Whose place is this?"

"Just under the Dodecanese." She gasped a little at the distance they had come while she was sleeping. "This is my own island. I purchased it privately. As far as I know, no one knows I am the owner. It is called Erimos."

"What does that mean? Does it mean Heaven On Earth?" She laughed.

"Almost. It is the Greek for wilderness. It also suggests solitude."

Julia set her hat and bag on the little table under the pergola, and they stepped from under the dappled shade into blinding sunlight. She walked to the low wall, looking out at the expanse of sparkling water. In the distance a cruise ship was just disappearing over the horizon. "Is there really no one out there with a telephoto lens?"

"This is a very small island in the middle of a pretty empty stretch of sea. However, there is a patrol boat circling the island. It will ensure that no vessel comes within two miles of us, whether by mistake or design."

Julia smiled up at him, a look that made his stomach tighten. "And how can they guarantee that some determined journalist won't simply ignore their orders and elude them?"

"There are five men aboard. They were chosen for this job partly because they are all very dark and swarthy examples of the Arab race."

Julia hiccuped into delighted laughter. "That," she accused, "sounds like cynical manipulation!"

"None of my men will *announce* that they are deranged terrorists who think nothing of committing murder on the high seas," he informed her in mock-innocent protest. "If people should happen to draw that conclusion, is that my fault—or their own acceptance of racial stereotyping?"

She sighed and more tension escaped on the gentle breeze. "I'm not going to think about it. I'm just going to enjoy these few hours of marvellous, luxurious, unbelievable peace and solitude!"

He cast a look at her that she couldn't read, then turned towards the house. "Shall we have lunch?"

Julia took a step and then stopped. "Oh!" she cried. "Who's going to prepare it?"

He glanced down at her. "Can't you cook, Julia?"

"No! Well—not very well."

"Then I will prepare our meals," said Rashid calmly. "Come."

The villa was small. From the main doors on the terrace they entered a large central hall with another door in the opposite wall leading out back to the orchard. On each side were doors leading to other rooms. There was a broad staircase leading up.

"Would you like to look around while I see to our lunch?" he asked.

She nodded. Rashid reached to the left and opened the door near the foot of the stairs for her.

"Make yourself at home," he invited, then moved in the other direction and went through a door on the opposite side of the hall.

She stepped into a broad, sprawling dining-cum-sitting room furnished in casually comfortable style with stuffed sofas and chairs and plump cushions. Greek kilims were tossed here and there over the tiled floor. A few pillars supported the ceiling. There was a big open fireplace carved into the wall. Beyond this room was a small room furnished as a study.

She returned to the hall. Upstairs there were several bedrooms—charming in their simplicity, but with stunning views out the windows and from a balcony. The bathroom was far from luxurious, though Julia was relieved to see it had one tap with running water. There was a small bathtub and a toilet, both of which were apparently operated by means of the bucket sitting by the tap. The shower was attached to a hose that could be screwed to the tap.

She wandered around, delighting in the solitude, the knowledge that they were completely alone, the complete lack of the sound—ever-present at home—of softly padding feet as staff whisked in and out.

She daydreamed of what her life might have been if she had been allowed to live a civilian life, like Christina. She would have a career. She might have married a man she loved and be pregnant with his child, and live in a place like this.

She might even be able to cook.

Downstairs on the other side of the hall was a very simple kitchen, in which there was nothing at all modern. Rashid was busy chopping fresh vegetables. Beyond the kitchen were several pantry-type rooms, and then a small set of rooms for a housekeeper.

When she returned to the kitchen Rashid was laying a tray with dishes and cutlery.

"This place is lovely!" she exclaimed. "It's so—*simple.*" Julia had grown up surrounded by luxury. She had attended exclusive schools, and her fellow students had been from among royalty and the world's wealthy. All her friends were surrounded by visible signs of privilege.

So perhaps it was only natural that she should take delight in a place so perfectly plain and basic, and yet he knew many women who would have turned up their noses in outrage if he had brought them here. He hadn't been sure how Julia would take it.

"I'm glad you like it," he said. "Where would you like to eat—on the terrace, or in the dining room?"

"Oh—the terrace," she said instantly. "That wonderful breeze!"

"Then perhaps you will take this tray and go and set the table there." It was said easily, but there was an air of command behind the tone that said he was a man used to leadership and comfortable with it.

She cleared the small table under the pergola, and set the plates and cutlery on it, to the music of the sea. Julia hummed a nameless tune as she worked, not asking herself what she was feeling.

She stood back to admire the little table when she had finished, and thought how rarely she had ever performed this ordinary task. Not during her marriage, certainly. Luigi had never been a man for intimate meals or holidays.

She went back into the kitchen and began to open cupboards.

Rashid, putting the last touches to lunch, glanced at her but left her to her own devices. She quickly found what she was looking for—a pretty brown pottery jug. She bent to fill it at the tap and then returned to the terrace.

When Rashid came out, pushing a trolley laden with food, the jug was in the centre of the table, filled with blossoms. He glanced at it and then at Julia, and nodded.

"Very nice," he said.

She felt a little thrill of pride. It wasn't the same as hearing her father's thanks for a meeting well run, or some effective advice, or the way she had handled some difficult person...but she didn't know what made it so different. Maybe because it was something she had done with her hands and her heart instead of her voice and her head.

Chapter 6

They sat, and Rashid offered her the food he had prepared. It looked deliciously simple—a couple of salads, feta cheese, herbs, and bread. Julia realized she was ravenous, and fell to.

"Did you build this house?" she asked, when she had eaten enough to quell the immediate pangs.

"No, it was here when I bought the island. It was once owned by a famous Greek writer, who came here to write for nearly forty years. When it came on the market after his death of course it was worth much more than when he had acquired it. The island has water, which is a very big advantage not shared by all the small islands."

"And you weren't moved to tear this down and build something more luxurious? Most people would."

"I wanted it for my own retreat, and I wanted to keep it as a place that did not require staff to run. This house is built to survive. And I like the atmosphere."

She knew what he meant. The house had a restful air,

and a kind of lightness. Her spirit seemed to lift just being here.

Julia looked around and sighed. "Wouldn't it be nice to be able to live here forever? Don't you sometimes wish you could just throw it all up and come and live here like an ordinary person?"

He was watching her gravely. "Yes, sometimes. But there is a job to do and fate has assigned it to me. I cannot simply turn my back on my country and the people. For my brother Hassan, it's different. He can escape most of the duties and obligations that come with being born to rule. He will only rule if I die without an heir."

She was chewing a delicious mouthful, and for a moment could only nod. She swallowed. "Like me and Christina." The tension in her stomach told her they were approaching dangerous territory.

But he seemed to feel that now was not the right moment. "I could be almost self-sufficient here—in summer, anyway. The orchard provides fruit, and there is a vegetable garden, but it requires watering by hand. That means someone has to come here regularly in the season."

"Don't you think you could find someone who would be happy to live here permanently and look after the place?"

"Yes, there are many people who seek out periods of isolation. Writers and religious mystics, for example. But then I would find them here when I came. Someday this may be a practical solution. At the moment, no."

"Where did the food we're eating come from?" she wanted to know. "Your garden?"

"It came in with us in the helicopter."

If he thought she was asking the questions as a way of keeping off the dangerous subject they had come here to discuss, he showed no sign of it. Nor any impatience. They had a long, leisurely meal, during which, to her relief, the subject of marriage never came up. They gossiped about the international figures they had both met, monarchs and presidents, writers and actresses.

He made her laugh with stories of diplomatic gaffes and blunders, and foreigners' misunderstanding of Tamiri culture.

"In my grandfather's day, and even into my father's, it was quite common for the palace to receive a special instruction, in advance of some notable's visit, that they should *not* be offered the sheep's eyes at dinner!" he said.

"Well," Julia retorted, "you'd certainly have had that request from *me* if I'd ever done a formal visit to Tamir. I can't imagine why anyone would consider sheep's eyes a delicacy."

Rashid laughed. "But that is the joke, Julia! We don't! We never did!"

"Oh, come on, everyone knows that sheep's eyes are a big deal in Arab countries! You make a special presentation of them to the guest of honour."

He lay back in his chair, his eyes alight with humour. "We present the sheep's eyes to the guest of honour as proof that the meat he is about to be served is freshly killed. It is the equivalent of showing someone the label on a bottle of wine before opening it. Don't you know that the freshness of meat can be judged from the eyeballs?"

Julia's mouth was slowly dropping open. "Are you serious?" she demanded, the trembling smile that transformed her into an impish child beginning to tweak the corners of her mouth. "Is this true?"

He lifted his hands from the arms of his chair and turned them palm up. "Of course it is true! Who in their right mind eats sheep's eyes? They are unpleasantly gelatinous and almost without flavour. I tried one once as a child, to see."

"But then—how? I mean, the literature is full of foreigners doing the stoic thing and swallowing eyeballs so as not to offend!"

"Can't you see how it would have happened? There you are, with an important foreigner in your tent or palace. Like a good host, you have ordered a sheep to be killed and roasted. Your cook brings you the eyeballs to examine. You are a wealthy man, with many sheep and nothing to hide, and you grandly signal to him to offer the evidence instead to your honoured guest.

"To your amazement, your guest picks up the eyes, one by one, and pops them in his mouth, eating them with every sign of delight and enjoyment. 'Ah, excellent.'" He mimicked a British accent, a man smiling to hide the fact that he is gagging, and Julia collapsed with laughter. "'Delicious, Sheikh Mohammad! Thank you! Delighted, I'm sure!'

"Of course, after a few such incidents, everyone understood that foreigners considered sheep's eyes a delicacy. It followed that this delicacy should be served to them whenever possible."

"It can't have been that way!" Julia protested.

"I assure you. In fact, in the palace in Tamir there is an old diary that records this peculiar culinary habit of the English, and mentions the writer's horror on the occasion when a generous foreigner insisted on sharing the delicacy with him—one eye each."

Julia laughed and mimed disgust, one hand to her throat. "Ugh! Oh don't, just the thought is making me gag! Thank God I'm not still having morning sickness! I'm not sure I believe this! I'm sure sheep's eyes were a legitimate delicacy in lots of Arab countries, if not Tamir."

"Perhaps eventually they became so in some areas. In the same way that sunglasses are an essential fashion accessory to the young in Tamir. Once the great and good take up a thing, it becomes the fashion everywhere. The British were very powerful in this region. However strange they appeared to us, the Arab people naturally adopted some of their customs. As the Montebellans did."

She smiled and shook her head, still half believing he was playing with her.

They had talked away a large part of the afternoon and Julia knew they would soon have to get down to business. She wasn't looking forward to arguing with him.

He got to his feet and extended a hand. "Come," he commanded softly, in a voice that she had to obey.

She stood up without a word. For a moment he hesitated. "Let's walk," he said, reaching for her hat and handing it to her. He drew her across the terrace and out through the gate, and together they walked down to the little cove. The sea breeze blew on her face, cooling her, though the sun was still hot.

"The water looks so inviting," she murmured. It was a tiny, perfect little bay, with crystal-clear water bubbling up onto the sand. Julia slipped out of her sandals and stepped into a receding wave. It trickled over her toes as it left, then rushed back up the sand to her again.

It was a seventh wave, larger and more powerful than previous ones, and Julia quickly snatched up the long full skirt of her dress as the wave piled up over her ankles.

Laughing with pleasure, she pulled her skirt up higher and stepped further into the delicious water. Under the water the sand dipped suddenly from shin to knee depth, and Julia screeched and waved her arm as she fought to retain her balance. The next wave rushed at her and toppled her.

She went down laughing, and was struggling to her feet

again in the bubbling water when Rashid's hand came down in support. She clasped it and came upright, water streaming from her hair and soaked dress. The wet cotton was plastered to her body.

Rashid's canvas shoes were soaked, and the legs of his white cotton pants. Behind him a wave drove her hat tumbling up the beach.

"My mother has a saying," Julia told him gravely.

"Which is?"

"'In for a penny, in for a pound,'" she said, and pushed his chest, hoping to topple him.

But he was very firmly grounded. It was like pushing a rock. Rashid smiled at her and shook his head as his chest absorbed the impact. His arms came up around her.

She was laughing. The corners of her full mouth were turned impishly up. Her eyelashes and her dark hair were sparkling with a thousand diamond droplets. The dress was plastered to the small, full breasts whose shape and warmth he knew so well, and yet not well enough. Its fabric clung to her abdomen and thighs, unmistakably female in their curves.

He had waited so long. All through the months of his self-imposed exile he had thought of Julia. Had dreamed of her, even. Had become half-obsessed.

And she was here, in his arms.

"Do you want to knock me off my feet, Julia?" he grated in her ear, passion making his voice rough when he meant it to be gentle. "You already do that."

Time slowed. Waves swirled up the sand around their feet and burbled against rocks before being sucked back into the oneness of the sea. Sand rasped across her feet. She felt the delicate tap of a tiny, fragile shell against her ankle.

His arms wrapped her tightly. He gazed down into her

upturned face as if searching a flower for a secret, so that his eyes were at once gentle and piercing. Unwilling to hurt her, and yet needing to know.

Her smile trembled across her full lips, tweaking the corners, as she returned his look. His hand threaded through her wet, wildly tangled hair, to cup her head.

"Did you dream of it?" he demanded, his voice rough.

She swallowed. "Dream?"

"My arms, my kiss. That time of madness—too short!—that we had together. Did you dream of it afterwards?"

She opened her mouth on a little gasp. "I—"

His arms shook her impatiently. "Tell me. I want to hear it."

Dream of him? She had relived the moment over and over, dreaming and waking. How he had kissed her, held her... *Rashid Kamal,* she had whispered in horror, and he had murmured, *Never mind.*

But to tell him so—!

"I dreamed of you," he said, his voice husky. "Your voice, your eyes, your scent...your body opening to me like a rose. *Warda.* A single, perfect rose. How perfect I did not know until I entered."

Her breath made a tiny gasp. Her throat closed. She couldn't speak.

"There was a moment—on our mission—when the danger was all around us, invisible, choking. We could smell it, but not see it. Those are the worst times. Danger that can be seen, can be touched, is easy. Fighting is easy. It is the waiting, the listening, the sniffing for danger, every pore open to take in information! That is the difficult part."

She murmured something inarticulate.

"I smelled you. Out of nowhere, your perfume. Your body. The scent of our bodies together."

A wave rushed at them, bubbling over their ankles with

a seductive roar, smashing into the rocks and splattering upward in a thousand blinding sparkles before dropping onto the sand and rushing back into the sea.

Human life is like this, Julia heard the wave whisper, and wondered distantly what there was about this moment that should bring her to that strange understanding. A brief moment of separation and individual sparkle, and then absorption into the great Oneness.

"We have a poem," he said. "Written about a woman who cannot visit her lover.

> *"Three things forever hinder her to visit us, for fear*
> *Of the intriguing spy or rancorous envier—*
> *Her forehead's lustre,*
> *and the sound of all her ornaments,*
> *And the sweet scent her creases hold*
> *of ambergris and myrrh.*
> *Grant that she doff her ornaments,*
> *and with her sleeve do hide*
> *Her brow...yet how shall she do her scent*
> *away from her?"*

Rashid stroked her tangled hair, and down her back over the already drying fabric of her dress.

"Even if I lost the memory of the sight of you, or the sound of your cries...your smell is mine."

His dark eyes were hungry as he bent and claimed her lips. Sweetness flowed out from his kiss into every cell of her being, and she felt her body melt for him, as it had once before, making her helpless to resist.

His hands were firm, pressing and stroking, as if by memorizing her body he could own it. He sank down onto the sand and drew her after him. She lay on his chest and looked into his eyes as Rashid combed her wet hair with strong, tender fingers.

They smiled without speaking. Just for this one moment, it seemed safe to forget who she was, who he was. Forget past, and future, and be in the now.

A wave came skittering up the sand under them, another seventh wave, and her wet dress lifted and was caught in the breeze. His hand trailed like water up the length of her thigh, over her hip, to her waist.

Her hair fell beside his face in damp sexy tangles, and his fingers threaded through it and pulled her face down again for his kiss. Her mouth was soft, yielding, and parted willingly for him, and passion flared in him so that he grunted, opening his mouth in the powerful hunger remembered from before.

As if he had frightened her, she lifted her head. "Rashid," she whispered protestingly.

"I want to make love to you, Julia," he said hoarsely. "I want to be inside you again. Tell me that you want it, too. Tell me that you remember my touch with pleasure."

She couldn't speak. Afraid of the truth, afraid of a lie. She licked her sun-hot lips and gazed at him.

He lifted his head and kissed her neck, in the tender place where it met her shoulder. He felt her tremble.

"Is that my answer? Shall I take my reading from your body, and not your words?" He watched her intently, and she felt the touch of his glance like a flame. Her eyelids drooped and he smiled.

"Take this off. I want to see you," he commanded. He pulled at her dress, and it was impossible to resist what she felt. He slid the fabric up her body, over her arms and head, and tossed it away. It left her naked except for a tiny pair of briefs.

Her skin was softly brown, highlighting the paler mounds

of her breasts. He leaned up on one elbow and looked down at the unmistakable female curves. His strong hand traced them then, slowly and firmly, as if to memorize them. The long, beautifully shaped legs, her rounded hips, the slight swell of her abdomen, the full breasts, gracefully curved arms, the long neck, the shell ears… His thumb stroked her moist lips, his fingers her cheek, temple, eyelid, and her hair again.

Sand clung to her at hip and thigh and shoulder, clustered in the tangled hair, dusted one cheek. The water slid up under her back and receded, matching the stroking of his hands, as if man and nature were in collusion. It was cool now because she was heated, but Rashid's gaze and his touch licked over her like a flame. Together, the sea and his touch brought every atom of her to tingling life.

Then his hand moved between her thighs and firmly clasped the mound there, and he watched in satisfaction as her back arched to thrust herself against his hand, like a cat. "A Tamiri poet has called this 'a sachet of spices in a pouch of silk,'" he whispered, stroking her with tantalizing pressure.

"No other man has tasted your spices. Only I know the delicious scent of you. Isn't it so?"

Julia could hardly breathe. "Isn't it so?" he insisted, holding her possessively, his thumb creating delicious spirals of sensation in her. "Tell me, Julia!"

She swallowed. "Yes," she whispered.

She was burning and melting for him when he dragged off his own clothes at last and, his body gleaming with water and sunshine, lifted up to make her his.

Chapter 7

Afterwards they swam in the deliciously cool water. It was the first time she had ever dared to swim naked, and the freedom made her drunk. They came out of the water and bent to pick up their discarded clothes and hat. He slipped his arm around her as they walked up towards the house, and her body inclined to his in remembered gratitude.

The sun was setting. "Time for dinner," Rashid murmured, at exactly the moment Julia said, "Time to be getting back, I suppose."

He looked at her. "Shall we have something to eat first?"

She was reluctant for the day to end. Here on this island, she was not a princess and he was not her enemy. Back in the world, everything would change. "Can you fly in the dark?" she temporized.

"It will be dark in any case in half an hour. It won't make any difference."

So she relaxed and gave in. She followed him around

the side of the house to the back, where they rinsed their sand-covered clothes under the tap there, and threw them over the clothesline. Then they rinsed their feet before entering the main hall by the back door.

It was mysterious with shadows. He led her upstairs to the bathroom. After a quick shower, Julia wrapped herself in a rough, thick towel and followed the lampglow to a bedroom, where she found Rashid standing naked at the window, gazing out at the sunset sky. An oil lamp sat beside the bed.

He had not heard her barefoot approach, and she stood watching him for a moment. The long line of his back curved down into firmly muscled buttocks. His legs were slim but strong, his feet firm on the tiled floor. His skin had a warm glow by the lamplight.

"Your turn," she said softly, and Rashid turned, smiled, and went out.

It was the kind of simple intimacy she had never shared with Luigi, she reflected as she dried herself. He had never gone naked around her. Never expressed any interest in her own nakedness. The few times during their marriage when she had been naked in his presence, he had made her feel invisible. She didn't realize how painful that had been until now, when Rashid came back from his own shower and his eyes flicked her body with bated hunger.

It was like looking into the coals of a banked fire.

He crossed the room to the closet and opened the door. Several items of clothing were hanging inside. He flicked through them quickly, then drew one out. He tossed it on the bed. It was a white cotton kaftan.

"Put this on," he said. "Or there will be no dinner for the foreseeable future."

By the light of the lamp he saw the glisten of tears in her eyes.

"What is it?"

She shook her head as she pulled on the cream-coloured cotton. "Nothing. Just a thought."

He slipped a kaftan over his own head. When his head emerged he was watching her with a darkly intent look. "What thought? Regret?"

A little grunt of laughter escaped her, and she smiled and shook her head. "No."

He crossed the room to her. She turned and looked out the window. The sun had disappeared now. She heard an unknown bird singing its twilight song. The sea tumbled and shushed.

Such peace. She said, looking out, "Just remembering the bad times, that's all."

"Tell me about the bad times," he commanded softly.

In a halting voice, she tried to encompass five years of humiliated misery into a few short sentences. "You're the only man who ever made me feel desirable," she finished. "Am I desirable, Rashid? Or do you just—" *know how to do your duty, as Luigi said,* she was going to ask, but he bent and roughly took her lips with his, smothering the words.

"Desirable?" he growled, when he lifted his mouth again. She was swooning with sensation. He bent and picked her up off her feet, and carried her to the bed. "You are so much a woman you could make a man forget his name!"

She didn't know how much time had passed when she awoke. The lamp had been turned very low, and she could smell the delicious scent of food over a charcoal fire.

Julia stretched her body luxuriously under the light covering of the sheet. She felt whole again. In the long years of her marriage, she had cut off from her own sexuality in order to survive. She had believed that the severance was permanent.

A smile twitched her lips. Well, it hadn't been permanent. She had closed a door on that part of herself, that was all. And Rashid—she wasn't going to think of his last name, just for today—had opened the door with one twist of his expert hand....

"That smells delicious," she said, entering the kitchen.

On one side of the kitchen was a glowing charcoal grill where several skewers of cut vegetables were grilling over open flame, in the Greek way. Rashid was standing over them, a huge striped apron over his white kaftan. He flung a pinch of herbs into the flames as she entered, and a delicious odour rose up on the smoke. Dusting off his fingers, he looked up.

"Are you hungry?" he asked softly.

Julia blushed, but she held his gaze. "Ravenous."

"Good. Set the table. Everything is in that cupboard."

It was all so new to her. Not just the lack of maids, but the feeling of working together on small tasks. She wondered if it became unimportant when you did it every day. Did people get casual about such precious togetherness?

She found two glass globes with candles inside and carried them out to the terrace, then set the table by their light. In the darkness the sound of the sea was strong. Julia stood for a long moment gazing at the night. There was no moon. How different the stars seemed here, in such simple surroundings. In the palace in San Sebastian there were always electric lights, and music, and the feeling of people around. Too many people.

Rashid came out of the kitchen with a tray of steaming, delicious-smelling food. He set the platters on the table, then disappeared and returned with the lantern he had been cooking by in the kitchen. It was much brighter than the candles, and at first Julia thought he was dissatisfied with the level of the lighting. But he walked over and set the lantern down on the far side of the terrace.

She frowned in perplexity. "What's that, a little background glow?"

Rashid smiled as he came towards her. "That," he said, "is for the insects."

"What?"

"It makes sense, doesn't it? Insects are drawn to light. So we sit by candlelight and leave the bright light for them to enjoy."

Julia laughed aloud. Whatever happened after this, at least she would have one crazy, wonderful day to remember. As they settled in their chairs to eat, she asked, "When are we going back?"

Rashid shot the contents of a skewer onto her plate. "It will be better if we stay the night, Julia. I had forgotten that tonight is the new moon. It is very dark. The helicopter is equipped for night flying, but…"

She didn't argue. There were quite a few yachts out there equipped with heliports, and not everyone was sober at this hour. Accidents did happen at night. "All right," she agreed, and wondered if she was imagining a little release of tension in him. "I'll have to phone my father."

He nodded.

He served her with a small grilled fish that smelled utterly delicious. Julia fell on the food with gusto. Sex, it seemed, gave a person an appetite.

"Is it the air," she cried after the first couple of mouthfuls, "or are you just a brilliant chef? I haven't tasted anything so absolutely scrumptious for ages."

Rashid's dark eyes rested on her. "Perhaps it is a question of your own appetites."

Julia bit her lip and turned away to hide the rush of heat in her cheeks and thighs.

All around them the night was magical. The sound of the sea mingled with the sound of the breeze blowing through the leaves. The stars sparkled on the water, making their own music. A small creature rustled among some dry leaves.

Against this background their voices were soft and intimate inside the circle of light the candles made for them. Afterwards she couldn't remember half the things they had talked about. She was enthralled, as if under an enchantment.

He told her wonderful stories, but he also listened. The closest they came to any difficult subject was when she told him about the time she and Christina had put honey in the British Ambassador's hat.

"Papa was absolutely beside himself with fury," she recalled as they laughed together. "I've never seen him as angry as that until—" She broke off.

"Until you confessed that I had made you pregnant?" Rashid guessed.

She didn't answer. She didn't want any dangerous topics spoiling this night of nights. This was her time out of time. There was no one to see her, no one to remember. Only the two of them. Here she was not Princess Julia Sebastiani di Vitale Ferrelli. She was simply Julia. A woman spending the evening, and the night to come, with her lover. There were probably millions of women doing the same thing tonight, somewhere in the world, but if so, not one of them was more thrilled than Julia to be where she was.

When they finished eating she said impulsively, "Let's go down to the water," and Rashid agreed without a word.

It was a small bay; there wasn't much of a stretch for walking. She held up the skirt of her kaftan and let the water run over her feet, then tilted her head back and gazed up at the crystal-clear stars.

There was a strange, unfamiliar feeling in her chest, and with a little gasp Julia realized that it was happiness. After two years of an unsatisfactory engagement, five of a tormented marriage, a year of divorce, and then six months of Lucas being lost...she was tasting something she had forgotten the taste of. Had almost forgotten it existed.

Her body was alive. She stretched her arms out, palms up, and reached up, feeling for the sky. "So this is what freedom feels like," she murmured.

"Have you never tasted it before?" he asked. His voice was quiet, but he sounded shocked.

"No—well, almost. When I was accepted for admission to a film school in London. I was nineteen, and I really felt the world was my oyster."

The sea whispered up the sand in the silence. "You did not attend the school?"

"No." She was reluctant to speak of it. She didn't want the memory of her thwarted hopes and lousy marriage coming between her and happiness tonight. "Papa wanted me at home. Did you know Delia went to school in England?"

"Delia?"

"She was the Sebastiani princess your great-something-uncle Omar nearly married—remember?"

He laughed. "Yes, I remember, now that you remind me. But I have told you, this is not a story that consumes me. I knew she was in England when she died. Omar, too. I know only a little more than that."

It suddenly occurred to Julia that this was probably the first time a Kamal and a Sebastiani had talked calmly together since it happened. She was sorry to become a Sebastiani again. She'd rather have saved the discussion till they were off this magical island, but it was, after all, the reason they had come here.

"What is the story as the Kamals see it?"

He shook his head. "There isn't much to it. A marriage was agreed between the two houses. Omar was introduced to Delia and the two fell deeply in love. He gave her an heirloom ruby ring called Fatima's Tear. But before the engagement could be formally celebrated, Delia was suddenly sent off to England."

Julia stood with her feet in the Mediterranean and soft darkness all around her, and listened to the tale of another century. About a girl who had been allowed to go to England when she begged to.

"Omar followed her to England. He was appalled by what he saw of London society. He thought it profligate, and wanted to bring Delia home. But copper had just been discovered on the property that formed Delia's dowry, and the Sebastianis astonished the Kamals by trying to break off the engagement. Omar and his father refused. Shortly afterwards Omar was dead. He had been shot. Delia died shortly afterwards, from grief."

Julia was amazed. "But that's so different from the version I heard!" she exclaimed.

Rashid laughed. "Does that surprise you? Even eyewitness reports are notoriously unreliable, an hour after the event. After one hundred years of oral tradition on each side, it would be a wonder if any of the elements remained recognizable, I imagine. What is the story the Sebastianis tell themselves?"

"The basic story I heard as a child is just that Omar was killed in England by highway robbers. The English police—Scotland Yard, I guess—said so. Delia died of grief, as you say. The family knew it was suicide, but it was hushed up completely at the time. Then, while the family was still in deep mourning, the Kamals trumped up the accusation of murder in order to be able to claim that the dowry land rightfully still belonged to them. Because of the copper that had been discovered on it, they didn't want to let it go."

Rashid laughed and sat down on a convenient rock. "All the elements of a good feud."

"I've been looking it up in the palace archives a bit lately," Julia told him. "The discovery of copper was quite a big thing then, a bit like discovering oil now. Did you know that? Copper was essential for the telegraph lines and electricity of the new industrial age. And it was a huge find. Those mines on Delia's Land still aren't depleted, not by a long shot.

"But according to my father no one tried to break the engagement because of it."

Rashid's voice came softly out of the darkness. "Omar wrote a letter to his father shortly before he died, mentioning that Delia's two brothers had paid him a visit at his London house. They tried to convince him to break off the engagement. Within days of that visit, he was dead. There were two bullets in his body. One from a shotgun, one a handgun."

"Really?" That surprised her.

"I believe his letter is still in our records," Rashid said.

"I'd love to see it," Julia said dubiously. It was hard to believe that so significant a visit could be omitted from the Sebastiani version of the story. And yet... "Delia's brothers—my great-grandfather Ugo and his brother, Julius—were actually in England around that time," she admitted. "They attended Sandhurst Military Academy. It was a Sebastiani family tradition. Papa even went. Lucas was the first Sebastiani not to be sent there for generations."

A seventh wave rushed up the sand in the silence, and

splashed on the rock where he was sitting. *What a strange thing the past is,* Julia thought. *Here and not here.*

Rashid grunted, as if his curiosity had now been sparked against his will.

"You have been looking into this recently?"

She felt suddenly awkward, and was glad there was no moon. She stirred the wet sand with a toe. "Yes, well—I suddenly realized I've never really known anything but the basic word-of-mouth story I just told you. But the palace archive has family correspondence and papers going back ages. I found out lots of stuff I didn't know.

"Delia was at school in England, too. A posh kind of finishing school, as far as I can gather. And she made friends there with a duke's daughter, named Elizabeth. Elizabeth came to Montebello for a visit when they left school. It was then that Delia and Omar got engaged."

She pulled up the skirt of her dress and paddled in the softly rushing waves. He asked, "And why did she go back to England?"

"Because Elizabeth's mother, the duchess, offered to chaperone her debut into English society along with Elizabeth, and present her at court and all that."

"Interesting. In our version it is said that Delia was torn from Omar and sent to England against her will."

"Oh no, that part at least can't be true! I've read that in a letter to one of her brothers. A formal debut was really a big thing in Victorian times, apparently. Delia had begged her father practically on her knees to let her go. She was beside herself with joy when he finally said yes. She actually wept for happiness. She points out where a tear has blotted her ink."

"That sounds odd for a girl who was deeply in love with her fiancé," he offered mildly.

"Well, I guess it really was a big thing. She'd have been presented to Queen Victoria, after all."

Rashid straightened and clasped her arms. Stars were reflected in his eyes as she gazed up into his shadowed face. "If this contradiction between two versions of the same event does not convince you, Julia, that the feud that divides our families is based on distorted facts and irrational emotion…"

But she didn't want her magical night wrecked by the discussion that had to come. "Let's go in, Rashid," she begged. "I'm so tired."

He held her for a long, impatient moment, then shook his head and dropped his hands. He turned. "All right," he said, and they turned back towards the house.

Overhead a satellite inscribed its arc beneath the stars. A cruise ship, brightly lit against the night, sailed by in the distance, where the blackness of sea and sky mingled into one.

The lantern on the terrace was a beacon, guiding them home.

Chapter 8

"**O**w!"

The cotton sheet scratched Julia's skin as she rolled over, bringing her awake. The morning sun was slanting in through the shutters and a shaft of light fell across Rashid's dark hair. He was awake, watching her.

Her thigh was suddenly itchy, and she reached down to scratch, but stopped after the first scrape of her nails on the tender flesh. "Ow!" she murmured again. And then, as he reached a lazy hand to her, "Oh, please, don't touch me!"

Rashid's eyebrows shot up. "You've conceived a distaste for me overnight?" he asked with a grin that reminded her how impossible that would be.

Gingerly she lifted the sheet. "I've got sunburn!" Her skin felt parched and tender.

Rashid sat up. "This could be unfortunate."

She felt a little shy as he drew back the sheet to examine her body. "Not severe," he announced after a moment. "You didn't put on sun cream yesterday?"

"I can't, I'm allergic to it. I come up in nasty little spots. I used to think it was the sun. Now I'm just very careful with exposure. Usually," she added with a grimace.

"Can you use body cream?" he asked.

"Oh, yes."

"I'll get some."

He slipped out from under the sheet. He had an erection, and Julia caught her breath at the still unfamiliar sight.

He looked down at her. "Do you expect the sight of your body in my bed to leave me unmoved?"

"I'm sorry," she said guiltily. "But I really don't think we'll be able to make love when my skin feels like this."

Rashid smiled and shook his head. "There are many ways of making love, Julia."

Her stomach clenched with melting anticipation. "Are there?" she breathed.

"And it will be my pleasure to teach them all to you, one by one."

He went out and returned a moment later with a blue squeeze bottle of after-sun "milk" and a large towel, which he laid on the little sofa bed sitting against a wall. "Lie on your front," he commanded softly, dragging it forward into the room.

Between her skin and her imagination, Julia was already on fire. She got up, crossed to the sofa bed, and lay face down on the towel without a word, her blood buzzing. She folded her hands under her cheek and closed her eyes.

The first cool squirt of the light liquid on her upper back was instantly soothing. And Rashid's touch was gentle. He began stroking it over her neck and shoulders, her arms, her hands. He stroked it on every inch of skin, and into every crease, shooting more out of the bottle at intervals.

"Your skin is only a little red," he remarked as he drew his hands in long smooth strokes down the length of her back. "Here is the worst." He wrapped both hands around her buttocks. "Here you were white, now pink. You have not before sunbathed naked?"

"No. You never know when some paparazzo has got a telephoto lens pointed your way, do you?" she said dreamily. His hands were stroking her bottom and thighs, and spirals of sweetness were lazily twisting out through her body.

"You were a virgin in more ways than one, then. This pleases a man, to be the first to teach a woman pleasure. Do you know it?"

"I guess so," Julia muttered, wondering if he knew what he was doing to her. He was an expert. He must know. Yet he seemed so casual, so matter-of-fact. Not like someone trying to seduce someone.

"Spread your legs for me," he commanded softly. She drew in an audible breath and obeyed. His hands slipped up the inside of her thighs and stroked cream into the folds, igniting little fires in her. By the time his hands left her thighs she was on the point of begging to be made love to, sunburn or no sunburn.

She felt him make two little puddles of cream on the backs of her knees, and he drew both hands down to her feet and slathered her ankles and soles and toes. Then back up to her thighs.

"You have not spread your legs enough," he complained firmly. "Wider."

He pressed her thighs apart till she was effectively straddling the narrow sofa bed, and her toes touched the floor. Then his hand slipped between her thighs to the sachet of spices in the pouch of silk, and his fingers toyed tantalizingly with the soft folds of flesh.

"This has no sunburn, you see," he said, as he drew his fingers up and down. "And here. No sunburn here." His finger slipped into the moist warmth inside her. "Lift up," he commanded.

She was beyond anything except abject obedience. The pleasure his touch gave her made her speechless. She pressed her feet to the floor and lifted her hips from the bed, making her body more accessible to him. At once he slipped his other hand under her, cupping her.

"Do you see how you fit into my hand?" he murmured. Now he stroked her from two directions, his finger moving to vibrate her body against the hand that cupped her.

Burning pleasure exploded in her, and she pressed into his hand as he ruthlessly continued to stroke and caress her, her body yearning for another release.

When it came, she moaned aloud. He rode the wave of her pleasure till it subsided, then lifted his hands. "Turn over."

She mutely obeyed, and he began again with the after-sun cream, though by this time she was beyond feeling pain from her wholly alive skin. He started with her face, gently soothing her forehead, nose, cheeks, lips. Then down her throat, to her shoulders, and then to her pale breasts.

The cool cream made her breasts shiver and become sensitive to the slightly rough skin of his palms. Julia was trembling both with the aftermath of pleasure and the anticipation that was building again, as he drew his hands across her stomach, her abdomen, gently stroking the swelling that marked where the baby lay hidden.

Then down to her mound, her thighs.

She couldn't stop her body pushing against his hand, hungry for more, but he only drew his hands down to her knees, squirted more cream there, and continued down her shins and the tops of her feet.

Then there was a pause as he set the plastic bottle to one side. Her eyes half opened. He was standing at the foot of the sofa, bending over her. He was firmly aroused, his flesh strong and heavy against his abdomen, and she nearly fainted with the kick of anticipation that assailed her.

"Open your legs," he said. He put his hands on her hips as she obeyed, and drew her body down till her feet were square on the floor and her hips rested on the edge of the bed. He sank down on the floor and pressed her knees apart, exposing her body to him.

Julia felt completely helpless, as if she were dependent on him not merely for pleasure, but for life. Her breath caught as his hands slid up from her knees and along her thighs, then pressed her legs even further apart.

Then his tongue pressed against her, rasping the sensitive bud so that she gasped aloud. He lifted his head and his gaze lazily met hers. "This is why they call it the sachet of spices," he said.

His mouth seemed to know everything about her. She writhed and cried out as it played over her flesh, and then the rasping went on and on and she exploded once, and again, and again. She sobbed with more pleasure than she had ever experienced in her life, more than she had dreamed existed.

When he lifted his head, she whispered, "Oh, how delicious, how sweet! Oh, thank you!"

"Did you think you had experienced the best of it, Julia?" he asked, reading her surprise. "But a virgin takes time to discover all the paths of pleasure in her body. Your body has more than this to learn. Stand up."

She wordlessly obeyed. He drew her to the end of the sofa bed, turned her around, and made her straddle it again. She bent over and rested her hands on the bed, her legs straight, so that she was totally exposed to him. She felt his hands clasp the front of her thighs.

"Is this comfortable for your skin, Julia?" he asked.

What on earth was he talking about? Comfortable? She was practically electrified over every square inch! Then she remembered—her sunburn.

She had to swallow before she could speak. "Yes," she whispered.

"Good," Rashid said, as one hand stroked the petals of her flesh and fitted his flesh to hers, and then, with a thrust that drove all the breath out of her body, he had sheathed himself in her.

She cried aloud, and so did he, and the sunlight seemed to dance around them as he pounded into her again. And again. Dimly she felt his hand shift, so that his finger again toyed with the little bundle of nerves that seemed like the centre of life to her. She exploded again, crying out with too much pleasure as he still drove into her.

His hands left her thighs and clenched on her bottom, pushing her flesh open to his gaze. "You are beautiful," he told her hoarsely. More pleasure shivered through her system as she turned her head and watched his face behind her. "Too beautiful, Julia!"

His hand stroked her towards another wild release, and he pounded into her desperately as pleasure built to a pitch in them both.

"Rashid!" she cried, as her excitement built almost to pain. The cry made him tremble. His pleasure was too much to contain. He dragged her against him, and she felt his flesh leap in her, heard him cry her name, as her own pleasure burst through and exploded with his in a wild sunburst of joy.

They breakfasted on fruit and coffee on the terrace, and Julia marvelled at how beautiful morning was. Like the first morning of the world.

After they had washed the dishes Rashid set her straw

hat on her head. Then he led her away from the house to another beach, a much longer stretch of sand, and they strolled barefoot along the water's edge as the sea, very gentle today, slipped up the white sand under their feet.

"This is paradise on earth," Julia murmured. And perhaps that mention was all it took for the serpent to gain entrance.

"We can come here often," he said. "My father depends on me more and more, but we are close enough here to be able to get back if there is any necessity. I do a certain amount of my paperwork here at the moment. That can be increased."

Julia looked at him. "What do you mean? Rashid, this can't continue. I can't keep seeing you."

He stopped and frowned at her. They were flanked by the pine forest now, and a breeze was stirring the branches into little whispers.

"What did you say?" he said, shaking his head as if he really hadn't heard.

She dropped her gaze. She didn't want to have this argument. Not now. But he was crazy if he really believed that anything permanent was possible between them. Sex didn't change anything.

Liar! a voice in her whispered. *Sex has changed you! That's not what I mean.*

"What time is it?" she demanded abruptly.

He shrugged. "About ten, probably."

"They were expecting me first thing this morning! I have to phone," she exclaimed.

"I have already spoken to your father."

Julia sucked in air with a surprised gasp. "Have you? What did you tell him?"

"That we had many things to discuss and you would not be back at the palace immediately."

''What does that mean? 'Not immediately'? We're going home this morning!''

He watched her. ''Possibly. It depends.''

For some reason she found herself evading a direct challenge of that. ''How did Papa take it?'' she asked.

''I am the father of your child, Julia,'' Rashid pointed out. ''We are two adults.''

''Nice if it works,'' she commented.

''Do not worry about your father. He knows he must give in to whatever decision you make.''

''Does he?'' she asked distantly. Whatever Rashid thought, it would kill her father if she married him. Which of course she wasn't going to do.

He did not know how Papa had looked when she told him the name of the man who had made her pregnant. Papa might not be saying anything now, but he had been almost as devastated by that as by the news of Lucas's disappearance.

His face had gone clay-coloured. She had never seen him look like that. *He raped you?*

Not rape, Papa. She couldn't look at him. *It wasn't rape.*

It wasn't rape? You are pregnant by Rashid Kamal and it was not rape? How can this be?

How she wished then that she had told him it was a stranger whose name she never learned. Anything but tell him that while her brother was missing, she had made love with a member of the family Papa believed responsible.

Papa—

Tell me no more! He had lifted his hands as if afraid to touch her suddenly. And then, in immediate contradiction, *For how long, Julia? How long have you been seeing this terrible man?*

Every part of it was shaming beyond belief. *I have*

never—we weren't—Papa, it just happened. And the look he had given her then would last all the rest of her life.

There had been worse to come, of course. The maid who had somehow been listening, who had whispered the story to someone who had whispered the story, until finally it was in the papers and Ahmed Kamal got hold of it....

The memory gave her the strength to challenge him. She said, "What do you mean, 'it depends'? I want to go home this morning. Now."

"Then we must have our discussion without delay."

"We don't really have anything to discuss." She wanted to get it over with.

His eyes glinted. "Good. Then we will return and be married as soon as it can be arranged. With Lucas...still missing, you will not want a grand occasion. We will postpone the state celebration. The people will und—"

She was breathless with the speed of it. "Stop!"

He looked a question.

"Marriage between us is out of the question. I told you. What do you imagine has changed?"

"Out of the question. Just like that." She saw the flash of his teeth, but he was not smiling. His eyes were black suddenly, with an emotion that almost frightened her.

"I will not marry you, Rashid."

He took a breath and showed her his teeth. "Then you will not be returning to Montebello this morning," he said. "You will not leave this island until you have promised to marry me."

Chapter 9

Julia's head whipped up, and the sun blinded her.

"You've got to be joking!"

"It is no joke."

"You're going to keep me here till I agree to fall in with your plans? I'm a hostage? A prisoner? That's why you brought me here?" She felt a thrill of fear. What a fool she had been to trust a Kamal, after all. What had possessed her to think him different from any of the others of that name? When had a Sebastiani ever been able to trust a Kamal?

"Not that exactly. I thought that you and I might deal better together if you were not surrounded by advisors."

"I'll bet!"

"I thought that if you had a chance to think it over calmly, you would understand that marriage is the best answer for us."

"I will never come to that conclusion. Are you out of your mind?"

He watched her steadily.

"How long do you intend to keep me here against my will?"

"It is not a question of that, Julia—"

"Like hell it isn't!" she cried furiously. "Answer my question! How long?"

The straw hat slipped off her head, unnoticed by both of them, and dropped down her back. It was held there as the loose knot in the scarf slowly gave way.

"I want us to discuss this in a sensible way, without worrying about the past," he said. "Cannot you see that it is time to put this ridiculous feud behind us?"

"How long?" she repeated stonily.

His jaw clenched. "Until you agree, at the very least, not to deny our engagement in the media."

"You want to brainwash me into doing something I am opposed to, both by inclination and principle. I will not agree. How long do you intend to keep trying before you give up? Are you going to starve me into submission? Beat me? Or just leave me here in solitary till I go mad?"

"You are being ridiculous, Julia! You know none of these things is in my mind," he exploded. "Why do you make so extreme a case?"

"Me?" she repeated, outraged. "You threaten my freedom and my right to self-determination and then blame *me* for making an extreme case?"

Her hat dropped to the sand and was caught by the breeze. It rolled down the beach and toppled, brim up, into a wave.

"You are pregnant with the child who will be my heir. Do you think I should have nothing to say about this?"

"I think you might try a more civilised way of saying it."

"No discussion was possible in Montebello. I brought you to neutral territory."

"Neutral, he calls it!"

"I will have you for my wife, Julia," he said in even tones.

"Not in this life!" she snapped.

"Why do you resist the only reasonable solution to this problem?"

"What problem?"

His eyes glinted dangerously. "Your pregnancy."

"And who told you that was a problem?" she demanded, in angry challenge.

"You are a princess. It cannot be right for you to have a child in this way."

"What century do you inhabit, Rashid? The whole world knows I'm pregnant. It's hardly going to surprise anybody when I have a baby!"

"The child needs a father. You need a husband."

This infuriated her. "I told you once before not to come charging into my life on your white horse! I will do just fine without you, thanks!"

He frowned at her. "Why are you taking this attitude?"

"It's not an attitude!" she cried angrily. "We are enemies. Pregnancy isn't going to change that."

"Wrong on three counts," he said grimly. "It is not 'a pregnancy,' Julia. It is a child. My son. And it will change everything, as children do. And I am not your enemy, however wrapped in ridiculous, outdated notions you have been in that palace. Do you think I can stand back and allow you to pass an ignorant prejudice against his father's family on to my son?"

She gasped under this onslaught. "I think you will stand back and watch me run my life as I see fit!" she declared.

"We made love once, Rashid! A one-night stand doesn't give you the right to—"

"Once? What was that we did this morning? And last night? And yesterday, on the beach? That was not making love?"

"Right! I see it now! You thought a little hot sex would help to change my mind about things!" she said, with bitter sarcasm. Shame crept slowly up from her gut, and she cringed from the knowledge of how easy a mark she had been. "Well, forget it! I may be susceptible, but I'm not stupid! I don't pay for sex with my freedom, thanks!"

"You are being offensive," he said through his teeth. He was absolutely furious.

"And you're not? Excuse me, but who brought whom to this island under false pretences?"

She couldn't believe it had all changed so suddenly. She had inhabited her paradise not even twenty-four hours.

"You degrade both yourself and me with such a suggestion. I made love to you with no such thought in mind."

"You never thought to soften up poor little deprived me with sex? *And there's more where that came from if you do as I say* never entered your thoughts?"

Rashid showed his teeth. "Of course I wanted to show you that a marriage between us could work on many levels."

"Political, territorial, and sexual."

"You were not unwilling, Julia. What was your own motive?"

"Motive? We're here in the middle of nowhere and there's no one to see or be hurt. But when we go back to our lives—"

"Is that what you believe? That this time together is a meaningless interval?" he demanded harshly. His eyes were boring into her.

"This is something I allowed myself. A time out of time."

"There is no time out of time for us. The clock is ticking."

She slumped. "Yes. I should have realized there's no such thing as a free lunch," she said. "I should have known you had an agenda."

"And you—you had no agenda? Why did you come here, Julia?"

She was silent. *For a taste of paradise,* she realized belatedly. *And that's what I got.* "You were the one who wanted to discuss things."

"You came here because there was nothing between us? To tell me that?"

She took a breath. "Stop trying to wrong foot me."

"You call it wrong footing you when I point out to you that we have more between us than what you so calmly call a one-night stand. Is that what it was? You were a virgin. It meant no more to you than a one-night stand?"

She felt cornered. "It's not something I think about—"

His hand snapped out and clasped her wrist. "Don't lie to me! You don't think of it? You are pregnant because of that night! Don't tell me you have forgotten it!"

"I didn't say that!" Julia cried. "What I was trying to say, if you would let me finish, is that I didn't—don't—" She broke off in exasperation at her inability to express herself, and pulled her hand away.

"There was no way to decide how it happened, that's what I mean! I had to stop blaming myself or go crazy. It wasn't a one-night stand, okay, you're right! But I don't know what it was. What came over me? It was because of Lucas, it was because I—damn it, I don't know why it happened!" she cried desperately. "But I've wished a million times that it hadn't!"

"Ah," Rashid said softly. "This is not something I have wished."

Something in his tone pulled at her, but she resisted.

"Well, and you're not the pregnant one, are you? But if you—if you knew what I did to my father when I got pregnant by a Kamal! Your father at least got some benefit out of this. He could start making demands for Delia's Land again. What did my father get? Nothing but humiliation."

He shook his head angrily. "This is not our fathers' business, Julia. It is yours and mine. We must settle it between us."

"Oh, sure. We'll duck down in the trenches, with our two families blasting away at each other over our heads."

"No. No longer. You do not see it yet, but a marriage between us will bring peace to our families. That is why it is so important. The child brings us together. He will inherit my family's throne. Marriage will unite us all."

She wasn't sure why she felt so deflated suddenly. She shook her head. "I told you before, Rashid. I'm not interested in another political marriage. And I'm sure as soon as you marry someone else and start having legitimate sons, people will forget any claims my child might have to the throne of Tamir. If your father hadn't made such a noise about it all, no one would ever have thought of this as a possibility."

"Do you think I would have had nothing to say about it?" he demanded incredulously.

Julia suddenly felt torn beyond endurance. She buried her face in her hands. "I don't know!" she cried. "I don't know. God, how I wish this had never happened! What evil luck was it that had you pass in the corridor that night in the château? Why didn't you just leave me there and pass by?"

A breeze sprang up, stirring her hair. The soft, sweet

scent of flowers brushed over them. Rashid suddenly saw that she was torn by every wind, like the roses.

"We get nowhere like this," he said. "Come, we will say no more about it now."

In the silence the waves washed up on the beach, rushed against the rocks. The sky was vivid blue and the sun was a white brand that hurt her. Julia felt her heart was breaking. She felt so weak. Another political marriage, was that what was in store for her? The difference would be that Rashid didn't find her sexually repulsive. But his heart would be no warmer.

Why was it her destiny not to be loved for herself? Why was she always to exchange the pledge of devotion of the marriage vow as a charade only? *Christina has found love,* she wanted to cry to the heavens. *Why can't I?* Much as she had used to cry to her parents, *Christina doesn't have to! Why do I?* whenever her presence was required at some state function Christina and Anna escaped.

"Not now, not ever. I am not going to marry you," she cried, tears cracking the smooth surface of her tone. "You didn't think of a child when you made love to me, and there's no reason for you to worry about him now."

He tried softness. "It is not merely the child, Julia—" he began, reaching for her.

She stood straight, out of his reach. "No, it's not just my child," she agreed. "You have a much bigger object in your sights than mere personal happiness, I know. Forgive me, Rashid, but I can't share that with you. Keep me here as long as it takes for that to sink in if you must. It won't change."

Her face looked very white under the tan, and in the bright sun her flesh seemed oddly translucent. She had a strong spirit, and powerful defences, and Rashid realized that this disguised her essential fragility. He felt a surge of protectiveness for her, but it was complicated by the fact that it was against himself that she now seemed to want protection.

"Come," he said. "The sun is too bright for you. Where is your hat? You should be under shade."

Her hands flying to her head, Julia noticed for the first time that her hat was missing. She turned and glanced around. Out on the water the straw hat skimmed the waves like a tiny vessel, running before the wind.

They landed on the palace lawn a few hours later. Julia jumped out and ran to a safe distance, expecting the helicopter to lift off again. Instead, the engine died completely. She turned in surprise.

Rashid stepped down and strode towards her. She shrugged. "You're coming in?"

"It is time I talked to your father."

"Does he have any say in the matter?"

"Your father can look after himself, Julia. He doesn't need you to protect him," he told her gently.

She was furious with him for putting her in this position. "You're sure of that."

The sun was bright in a clear sky. The palace looked beautiful with its white walls and pillars set against sweeping green lawns. Sunlight sparkled from the broad windows.

"Cooee! Your Highness! Princess Julia!"

They turned. Thirty yards away, pressed against the heavy wrought-iron gates of the palace's main entrance, several tourists waved and smiled. "Ooo, she's with him! She's actually with Prince Rashid!" a female voice cried. "Aren't they romantic together!"

"Congratulations!" a hearty voice called, and was echoed by several softer twitters.

Grinning broadly, Rashid bowed in acknowledgement. "Thank you!" he called, to the manifest delight of all the women.

"Will you stop flirting?" Julia muttered. "Come on, if you're insisting on this, let's get inside. We should have landed at the back." She led him across the lawn and around the side of the building.

"You don't use the main entrance?"

"Only on special or state occasions."

"You do not consider our first arrival here together worthy of such distinction?"

She eyed him. "As it's also our last, perhaps I should."

Rashid laughed. "Ah, Julia, has no one taught you not to tempt fate? You should say *insh'Allah* if you really mean it. It means 'if God wills.' But maybe—"

"*Insh'Allah,*" she repeated grimly. "If God wills, we are crossing this stretch of lawn together for the first and last time."

"I am sure He does not will it," Rashid retorted instantly.

The door opened before she could respond.

"Good afternoon, Your Royal Highness. Good afternoon, Your Royal Highness."

"Good afternoon, Graham." Gritting her teeth, she stepped past the butler and into the private foyer. "Where is my father, Graham?" she asked.

Graham did his best to remain imperturbable, which films and television had served to convince him butlers always were. But he was clearly very moved by the thought of the Crown Prince of Tamir being here in San Sebastian Palace.

"In the White Lounge, madame. May I say—" Julia opened her eyes at him, and he coughed. "May I just say

how delighted the staff are, madame? And sir.'' He bowed.
''We all wish you very great happiness.''

''I hope you don't believe *everything* you read in the
papers, Graham,'' Julia said waspishly.

His eyelids flickered. ''Oh, no, madame.''

Rashid, his hands in his pockets, was grinning. ''Thank
you, Graham. We appreciate your good wishes.''

She led Rashid into the family's favourite summer
lounge, a room painted and furnished in whites and creams.
It was a peaceful, comfortable room with huge windows
facing south over a mile-long stretch of lawn that ended in
cliffs overlooking the sea.

Her mother and father were sitting with the Sunday papers spread out around them. Julia gazed blankly at the
scene. After only a day and a half away, this scene seemed
like something out of another world.

Or perhaps it was she who was out of another world.
She felt changed. As if she might no longer speak a language her parents understood.

''Mama? Papa?'' They lifted their heads, gasped and
hurried to their feet. ''Prince Rashid is here.''

''My father will come around to the idea,'' Rashid was
saying calmly half an hour later, as they sat at lunch.

A stranger, Julia supposed, might have found it funny.
Her mother, beautiful and gracious, was being warmly en-
gaging, but not even a lie detector test could have sussed
out her real feelings. Her father, in what the family called
''His Majesty'' mode, was very gruff.

Rashid could consider himself lucky that he hadn't
drawn the ''Great Warrior'' card. That was Papa's killer
mode.

Gwendolyn had insisted that Rashid stay to luncheon,
though it was clear that King Marcus was not happy to be

eating bread and salt with a Kamal. And what was more, the queen ordered the meal served, not in the formal dining room, not even in the family dining room, but in the cosy and intimate little breakfast room off the White Lounge, where a small table overlooked a terrace, and where her parents had taken breakfast together virtually every morning for more than thirty-six years.

"He will, will he?" King Marcus harrumphed. He was looking inward at something none of them could see. It apparently wasn't very inspiring.

"When he realizes that it's inevitable, yes."

His Majesty grunted and drew himself up. Julia could almost see his ermine robes and the crown on the thick white waves of hair. His black eyes flashed majestic fire. "Seems to me that before it becomes inevitable you have to convince my daughter!"

Rashid smiled. "True. I'm making that my first priority."

Julia dropped her gaze into her lap, shaking her head.

"And how do you intend to do that, sir?"

Papa only ever called men "sir" like that when he was seriously displeased. Julia half smiled. At least Papa was on her side. Let Rashid try fighting His Majesty.

Rashid reached out and laid a possessive hand on her arm.

"I'll think of something," he promised softly. In spite of herself, she felt a little thrill of pleasure at his tone. It was almost like being wooed for herself. If you didn't know all he wanted was a political alliance, you could almost imagine he was in love.

"Pretty rich, to go chasing after a woman who's made it clear she doesn't want you," Marcus rapped out. "A man should take no for an answer."

There was a stifled shriek from her mother. "What?" she demanded, sitting up very straight.

Marcus flicked her a look. "Oh, well, you know what I—"

"A man should take no for an answer?" she repeated in amused indignation. "Exactly how many times did *you* refuse to take no for an answer, Marcus?"

His Majesty shifted uneasily. "Now, Gwen—"

"How many?"

"One or two, I suppose."

"Papa, you know the number perfectly well," Julia chided. She couldn't help giggling. This teasing was a sign that His Majesty had been routed.

"Three, was it? Anyway, I knew you didn't mean it."

Julia had been raised on the stories of their intense love affair and the numerous proposals her father had had to make before her mother had been convinced the marriage would work. She let her mind wander to a scenario where Rashid loved her like that. A jolt of excitement buzzed through her, and she bit her lip and hastily pulled her thoughts back to the here and now.

"Your masculine self-assurance wasn't quite so overwhelming at the time, I seem to remember," her mother was saying.

Papa gave Rashid a conspiratorial wink. "Go unshaven for a day or two, and—" he wiggled his fingers "—ruffle your hair a bit. That usually clinches it."

Rashid grinned. "I'll remember that."

And suddenly Rashid and Papa were on the same side of the fence. Julia looked at her mother with renewed respect. Gwendolyn could do most things, but Julia would never have believed even she would be able to pull off a thing like this.

Chapter 10

Rashid lifted the chopper up above the palace. The black, white and gold of the Montebellan flag snapped in the wind, as if it, too, were mocking his hopes. He banked and headed east.

He was feeling slightly shell-shocked. King Marcus had unbent with him, and by the time they had smoked cigars together in the palace garden, they'd understood each other pretty well. But Rashid wasn't making the mistake of thinking that the masculine camaraderie betokened his acceptance as prospective son-in-law. Marcus was still firmly opposed to the union—not that he'd said so.

Well, with his own father still demanding Delia's Land, what did he expect?

Opposition from King Marcus he had been sure of. What shook him was Julia's continued rejection.

As the handsome, rich, educated, polo-playing Crown Prince of a prosperous and happy nation, he was well aware that there were few women who would have rejected a proposal of marriage from him. Now that all three of the princes of the Barakat Emirates were happily married, the attention of the world's press was often focussed on him. He was used to hearing himself called "the world's most eligible prince."

If he had sat down and considered the matter for a week it would never have occurred to him that Julia would resent his defusing of the media speculation with the arbitrary announcement that they would marry, but that paled beside the fact that she was now adamantly refusing to marry him. What the devil was the matter with her? Why was she baulking at the obvious solution—one that solved not only her own immediate problem, that of her pregnancy, but also paved the way for peace between two nations?

She had said that she did not love him. He had not liked hearing it, of course. But perhaps that was only because it wasn't what he was used to hearing.

Julia was clearly going to be different from any other woman he knew. She was making up for a career lack of rejection all at once. When she was pregnant! When he had proved to them both how deep their physical attraction for each other went! He knew that she had never experienced anything like what they had shared on Erimos. And for a certainty he never had.

Maybe he should have seen their first encounter in the château as a forewarning. The madness that had overwhelmed him there had still never been satisfactorily explained. What had possessed them that night? For himself, he would have said that nothing on earth could have swayed him when he was about to embark on the most important mission in the modern history of his country. Certainly not sex with Princess Julia Sebastiani.

And as for Julia, he now saw how deep her prejudice against the Kamals was. And she had been a virgin, too.

Born Royal

She had had every reason to repudiate him the moment the light went on. There the mystery was equally unfathomable.

Perhaps the château was haunted. Most of them were. *Haunted by a ghost who likes sex?* he challenged himself dryly. *And is there a ghost on Erimos, too?*

As the three islands of Tamir came into view, he altered his course slightly and headed for the easternmost island, Siraj. What he needed to clear his head was a gallop.

He knew perfectly well that most of the women who professed deathless love for him were much more in love with his money and his position than himself. But still, it was a shock to have this beautiful woman, with whom he had shared such profound passion, and who was actually pregnant with his baby, declare so coolly, *I will not marry you because I do not love you.*

He was a little angry with her, he discovered. How did she know she would not fall in love with him? They had had so little time together. She had insisted on leaving Erimos, and when it came to it, of course he could not keep her there against her will. But if she had given him more time…

It was all too damned contradictory. She was an irritating woman. Rashid landed the helicopter on the heliport at his farm and jumped out with a quick word to the mechanic. Then he strode down to the stable.

Araby greeted him with his usual soft-nosed, whuffling pleasure, and Rashid absently slipped his hand into his jacket pocket, but he had no sugar there.

He patted the horse's nose and turned to the stable hand. "Saddle him," he ordered brusquely, then strode away to change.

He returned within ten minutes, took Araby's reins with a brief word, mounted and rode off. Riding was therapeutic for him, and he hoped it would soothe him this time. Araby needed little encouragement to break into a gallop.

This damned feud! Based on nothing but legend and hot air! It surprised him not in the least to discover that the Sebastianis had a totally different version of the events, but he still didn't give a damn about it. What difference did it make now who had killed Omar? Why couldn't they all forget it?

He shook his head. His father's dogged insistence on ownership of Delia's Land was a huge hurdle to forgetting, he had to face it. But there was a way out of this, if only he could find it. And maybe that way led through the feud, not around it. Both King Marcus and his own father had been steeped in the feud since birth, and Julia, too. He had to recognize that he wasn't going to win this merely by expecting people to forget. If Julia had agreed to the marriage, together they might have faced out the opposition. As it was...

As they approached the cliff edge, Rashid pulled his mount to a standstill and gazed absently down, where the sea pounded against a spread of black rocks.

He had believed it settled. This morning, after their passionate lovemaking, he had taken it for granted that she agreed that marriage was the way forward for them. When she had rejected him again...that had been a moment like nothing else he had ever experienced.

He thought of how long ago he had first conceived of his grand plan to marry Julia Sebastiani and forge a permanent peace. Her sudden engagement had taken him completely by surprise, and he had watched the slow progress to her marriage with irritated frustration. If she was going to marry the man, why didn't she do it? If not, why not break it off so that he could try...?

And then she had married. He had been consumed with

useless regret then. He should have acted, engagement or no engagement. It was a long time before he could forgive himself.

The horse whinnied and tossed his head, bringing Rashid back to the present. He shook his head in irritation. Julia was deeply attracted to him. She had not faked that wild sexual excitement. He thought of the way she had looked this morning, the feel of her skin under his hands, and felt his flesh stir painfully against the saddle.

He laughed. No, Julia hadn't faked it. Any more than he had.

He suddenly realized that it was all up to him. He had to find a way to make their marriage possible. Inevitable.

Julia Says NO!

Princess Julia will not marry Crown Prince Rashid Kamal, the *Montebello Messenger* has learned. "Prince Rashid's announcement was incorrect," the brief palace press release disclosed yesterday. "The princess has no plans to remarry in the foreseeable future."

It is widely believed that the star-crossed lovers have met with deep opposition from both King Marcus and King Ahmed. The rival monarchs are in bitter dispute over the ownership of the rich Montebello territory nicknamed "Delia's Land." The latest rift is the result of King Ahmed's renewed pressing of Tamir's claims to the land, source of an ancient dispute between the families.

"Julia and Rashid are obviously deeply in love," an informed source told the *Messenger*. "But that cuts no ice with their fathers."

Julia and Rashid are known to have confronted King Marcus at the palace in San Sebastian on Sunday, but the hoped-for permission was not forthcoming. That

King Ahmed has also voiced his disapproval is likely. Clearly the combined discouragement has been potent enough to destroy the couple's hopes of a quick resolution of their dilemma of the heart. *(More stories and comment on pages 3, 6, 7 and 28.)*

"So, now we are Romeo and Juliet?" Rashid's voice murmured in dry amusement when she answered the phone.

"That isn't the story we gave them," Julia protested, but without much heat. She knew she didn't have to explain to Rashid about the media, whatever else he didn't understand.

"Why did you say anything at all?"

"Does the name Erimos mean anything to you?"

He was silent.

"I didn't want to put you to the trouble of taking me prisoner again," she informed him sweetly. "I thought this would remove temptation. It's done. It's over with."

She really was in a mood, Julia discovered. For absolutely no reason. She felt like hitting someone. Or screaming. Or crying.

"Why could you not wait until—"

"Until what? Until it became a fact by virtue of never having been challenged?"

Until I've found a way around this, he wanted to say.

"There's a solution to this," he said.

Julia laughed angrily. "You're looking at it from the wrong direction, Rashid. The solution is, there's no problem in the first place!"

Alima Kamal looked at her son sadly.

"What do you want me to say, Rashid? You want a woman who does not appear to want you. You are not the first man to experience such a thing."

"It's not a case of unrequited love, Mother," he said
impatiently. "It's not just a question of going away and
licking my wounds and then finding another woman who
likes me better. Everything I have planned for Tamir hangs
on this marriage. I can't just let it go!"

His mother looked at him oddly. "Did you explain that
to Julia?"

"Yes! Over and over!"

She smiled sadly at her son's obtuseness. "Was Julia in
love with her former husband, do you know?"

"Not from the way she spoke. I can't see that it was an
important marriage politically, but she talked as if she'd
gone into it against her will."

"Is she in love with someone else?"

"No," he said quickly. His mother showed surprise at
his certainty, and he suddenly realized he had no proof of
that. She had been a virgin, but that didn't mean she wasn't
in love. "I doubt it. She'd have given that as a reason for
not marrying me, wouldn't she?"

"Maybe, maybe not. Wait here a moment."

He watched the shadows creep across the courtyard as
he waited for her to return. A fountain splashed gently,
catching the last rays of the sun. The mosaic tile surrounding the four neat channels that carried water to the fountain
glowed with the faded, painstaking patterns of another age.

Was Julia in love with someone else? His stomach
twisted. That really would wreck his plans, unless there was
a reason she couldn't marry the other man. A married man,
perhaps? He didn't like the idea. He didn't like to think
that she had maybe made love to him while thinking of
someone else. That would certainly explain her wild response, though, if she had been resisting an impossible passion for someone else…. *But her passion for me was also*

forbidden, he told himself, irritated by these ideas, *and she didn't resist that.*

His mother returned with a velvet jewellers' box, ring size. She put it on the table in front of him. "I wonder if you've ever seen that? I don't suppose you have."

He reached out curiously to pick up the faded little box and snapped it open. Inside was a ruby-and-diamond ring. "What is it?"

"That was Delia Sebastiani's engagement ring."

Rashid frowned. "How does it come to be in our possession, then?"

"The ring was returned by the Sebastianis after her tragic death. When King Mukhtar was demanding the dowry land in exchange for his son's life, King Augustus sent this with the message that the ring was all the Kamals would ever get from his kingdom. I imagine Omar's mother took possession of it. It's been passed down as an heirloom to the new bride of the Crown Prince ever since."

"Omar gave Delia this? I always understood he gave her one of the family jewels. This doesn't look like—"

"According to the story that came with the ring when your father's mother passed it on to me, he did. He gave her a solitaire ruby ring they called Fatima's Tear."

Rashid frowned down at the ring. It was a curiously clumsy arrangement, six small quarter-carat diamonds and two single-carat diamonds, he guessed, in a circle surrounding a pigeon's blood ruby. The ruby was larger, and sat proud of the rest of the setting. The diamonds were too big to make a comfortable setting for the ruby. It was not something any Tamiri court jeweller would have made. He glanced at the box. On the satin lining he could just read in gold lettering, "Barratt and Runyon, Jewellers, London."

He grunted in surprise. "He bought her another ring in London? What happened to Fatima's Tear?"

"My guess is that the stone in the centre is Fatima's Tear. For some reason it was reset with those diamonds in London."

Rashid was mystified. "Why, do you think?"

Queen Alima shrugged. "According to the story as I had it from your grandmother, Fatima's Tear was chosen as an engagement ring before Omar met Delia Sebastiani. When he met her, he fell deeply and passionately in love, on first sight. He gave her the ruby, but I've sometimes wondered if he felt it wasn't good enough to express what he felt."

Rashid lifted his eyebrows. His mother shrugged.

"Or perhaps, when he got to London, he discovered that engaged girls there were more often given diamonds, or something of that nature. Whatever it was, the ring—" she took it from his open palm and looked at it again "—seems to me a symbol of deep and abiding love."

She set it back in his hand and looked at her son. "Every woman wants to feel that kind of love from the man she marries. And she wants to return the feeling. And I don't believe men are as free from wishing for it as they like to pretend, either."

Rashid flipped the ring thoughtfully and caught it between his fingers. He looked at it. Both the diamonds and the ruby glowed with the deep inner light that only the finest precious stones had.

"If Julia is refusing to marry you as a way of settling the feud, Rashid, it may be because, in her heart, she still longs for that kind of all-consuming love. She is only twenty-nine, after all. It's by no means too late for her."

He was silent for a moment of staring at the glowing stones. The ring felt heavy, heavier than the actual weight. His mother was right. It had an emotional pull. It was somehow beautiful in spite of the strange mismatch of the stones.

"What are you saying? That I ought to let her alone so that she can go off and find that kind of love somewhere?"

Over my dead body, he thought involuntarily.

His mother smiled sadly. "I don't know what you should do, my son. By tradition I will pass that ring on to your wife, whoever she is, soon after your wedding day. Love is a powerful thing, Rashid, and marriage without it might not be so easy as you are imagining right now. Maybe *you* should be more determined to find a woman you can love the way Omar loved Delia."

His mother went inside, leaving him with the ring. Twilight fell over the courtyard. Rashid sat meditating, rolling the ring in his fingers, while his thoughts roamed over what his mother had said.

Love. Find a woman you can love.

He returned to the contemplation of the ring. It seemed unsuitable as an engagement ring. It had more the weight of a man's ring. The gold setting was thick and heavy.

Delia Sebastiani, by all accounts, had been a small, delicate woman. Like Julia, he imagined. If Omar had really chosen such an unsuitable ring for her, could it be true that he had loved her so devotedly? It wasn't the ring he would give Julia, certainly. As a dress ring, a woman might wear it, but if—when!—Julia accepted him, he would give her a ring to match her own grace....

Iqbal arrived silently, pushing the drinks trolley. He moved the length of the cloister, turning on a few soft lights, then the lamp at Rashid's elbow. He brushed the table with a tiny hand broom. Then he quietly set down several bowls of appetizers and fresh herbs, and stood patiently waiting.

Rashid came out of his trance. "Water, please, Iqbal," he said, setting the ring down as he reached for a sprig of basil. He popped the fresh greenery into his mouth and chewed pensively.

Then he absently reached for the ring again. He held the jewel under the lamp. It was a wonderful ruby. Rubies did show better when set with diamonds, but if ever he saw a ruby that could stand on its own, Fatima's Tear was it.

The whole thing was a mystery. Why reset an heirloom ring? Why not just buy a new one?

Iqbal placed a frosty glass of water with ice and a slice of lime in front of him. Rashid held up the jewel so that it sparkled in the lamplight.

"What do you make of that, Iqbal?"

The servant paused and looked at it. "A very handsome jewel, Prince. Is it rare?"

"Rare enough," Rashid agreed. "Suitable for a lady, do you think?"

Iqbal smiled involuntarily and picked up the ring as Rashid held it out. "For the princess? Has she—"

Rashid's frown cut him off. *Still not running smoothly, then,* Iqbal noted sadly. He couldn't understand the princess. What better man could she be hoping to find? He was a good master, Prince Rashid. The best. Everybody knew that a good master meant a good man. But it was clear from his face now that he had been deeply disappointed. Iqbal sighed.

"It is a beautiful ruby, isn't it?" he temporized. He turned it over and set it back on Rashid's palm. "What is the insignia?"

"Insignia?" Rashid held the ring to the light. Iqbal was right. On the underside of the setting was an engraving. A crest of some kind.

"That's not the Kamal mark," he murmured half to himself. "Nothing like it! A coat of arms?"

Iqbal, recognizing that he was no longer required, diplomatically retreated, leaving Rashid to the examination of the ring.

"Not the Sebastiani coat of arms, if so," Rashid told himself, twisting and turning the ring in the lamplight to get a better look. "Looks like something from European aristocracy."

He raised his head and stared into the night. "What the devil was Omar's fiancée doing with a foreign coat of arms on her engagement ring? Nothing makes sense!"

Rashid stood up and moved into the courtyard, where the fountain played. Its music helped him think. He gazed at the ring, his head buzzing....

"Son? Will you be coming in to dinner?"

Rashid surfaced from his reverie with a start. He had been staring at the ring in the gloom, completely unaware of his surroundings, as if he had been half in that other world, a century old.

"I'll be there in a minute."

There was a story behind this. There had to be more to it than anyone had previously guessed. And if no one had guessed it, no one had fully investigated.

Suppose the real truth surrounding Omar's murder could be unravelled at this late date? Suppose an investigation into the two contradictory family versions would reveal not that one was right and one wrong, but a third version altogether?

He was convinced that Julia was refusing to marry him largely because of the feud. Because his family had blamed her family for a murder of which the Sebastianis believed themselves innocent. And had used that accusation as the basis for claiming their land.

Suppose he found the truth? There was a truth, after all. Suppose he proved it, one way or the other—would that erase the feud between their families?

Would it allow Julia to marry him?

Chapter 11

"Are you crazy?" Julia demanded.

"Crazy with wanting you," he agreed. He was suddenly seeing her with new eyes. He wanted her, body and soul. "Do you think pleasure is addictive?"

His smile was both rueful and incredibly sexy. She pressed her lips together. "I wouldn't know!"

"Liar." He reached out and stroked her hair back from her brown cheek. They were sitting in the San Sebastian palace rose garden, at a table under the shade of a massive rose-clustered pergola. Beside them was a small pond. It looked very English, Rashid thought, and must have taken enormous work to produce. He wondered if Queen Gwendolyn was responsible, or if it was a throwback to the colonial period of Montebello.

"Can we talk about Delia and Omar, please? And about how you're going to discover the real truth?"

He nodded, still smiling. Then he stood and reached into

his pocket. He pulled out the jeweller's box and set it in front of her.

In automatic response, Julia picked it up and opened it. "Oh!" she cried, dropping the box as if it were hot. She glanced up at him and then back at the ring. "What's this?" she asked suspiciously. Was he trying to trap her? She glanced around nervously.

"That," he said, seating himself again and reaching for the box with one long, strong hand, "is Delia's engagement ring," and Julia lost all suspicion in surprise. Absently he plucked it out of the box, picked up Julia's hand, and slid it onto her right-hand ring finger. It slipped down over the knuckle, a perfect fit.

"Is it really?" she breathed, instantly enchanted. She lifted her hand to look more closely. "How do you come to have it?"

He told her the story his mother had told him. Julia's eyes got wide with interest as he proceeded, and by the end of his tale she had taken off the ring and was examining the engraving on the underside.

When he was finished, she sat gazing at him, all self-consciousness lost in the mystery. "So what's your idea of what happened?" she asked.

"Let's look at it," Rashid said. "A young princess becomes engaged to the prince of a neighbouring country. Her dowry is a substantial piece of land that her father owns privately. She is given an heirloom ring to seal the bargain.

"She is so in love with her fiancé that later, when he dies, she will kill herself in despair. But instead of proceeding to the marriage, the princess travels to London, where, officially, she is to make her debut and be presented at court.

"But a valuable mineral deposit has suddenly been discovered on the dowry land, and her fiancé suspects that she is actually being removed from his path so that the engagement can be broken and the dowry land retained. All right so far?''

"Yes," Julia commented. "Except that we didn't break the engagement."

"Of course. The prince, maddened by thwarted love, follows the princess to London. He has the heirloom ring reset in an inappropriate diamond setting. Some sort of coat of arms is then engraved on the underside of the ring.

"The prince writes home to his father about a visit the princess's two brothers make to him, seeking to break the engagement. The prince says he has refused. Within days, the prince's body is found by the roadside, with two bullets in it, from two different guns. The police call it a robbery gone wrong. Shortly afterwards, the princess kills herself."

Rashid leaned back in his chair. "Nothing makes sense," he said. "Nothing in that story adds up."

Julia gazed absently down at the ring. "Are you sure about all this? I mean, isn't it possible the ring came into the Kamal family complete with crest—maybe some foreign king gave it to someone? That wouldn't prevent it being called Fatima's Tear later, would it?"

Rashid shook his head. "I've looked it up in an old treasury listing. In a catalogue of 1817 Fatima's Tear is listed as a ring with a single ruby. No diamonds. No mention of any insignia, either."

She was already nodding before he finished. "I wonder whose coat of arms this is."

"I am sure there are ways of finding out."

Julia sat up. "You're right! And not a million miles from here, either! There must be a book of heraldry in the library."

Half an hour later the palace archivist reverently set an ancient leather-bound book in front of them. "This goes up to 1850,'' Arthur said, a little breathless from having heaved the massive volume down from a shelf. "If you want to include recently created titles, you will have to consult a later book. This one.'' He patted a small, neat, modern book as he set it down. "But I thought you might be interested in this old work for its own sake.''

They soon saw what he meant. The leather-bound antique, *Coats of Arms of the Noble Families of England, Scotland, Wales and Ireland,* devoted a page to each coat of arms, and each was intricately and beautifully painted on thick creamy vellum, with a sheet of onionskin to protect it. On the left of each was the description.

"It's stunning,'' Julia breathed as she carefully turned the pages. "But how are we ever going to pinpoint that tiny little engraving? Some of these are so similar to each other....''

Rashid was examining the engraving on the ring. "This animal looks like a deer,'' he offered.

Arthur's eyes lit up as he saw the ring. "You're trying to identify a specific coat of arms?'' he asked, as if life could hold no more exciting task. "May I?''

Rashid dropped the ring into his palm without a word and watched curiously as the archivist held it up to the light streaming down from a window high over a wall of bookshelves. "A magnifying glass, I think,'' Arthur murmured, disappearing back to his desk. A minute later he was sitting by a bright desk lamp, magnifying glass held over the ring.

"Crest seems to be a lion statant on a coronet...the arms quarterly...supporters difficult to be certain, as you say, maybe stag sinister...hmmm. Well, that gives us a start. Let's look for those first.''

Rashid laughed aloud. "Was that really English you were speaking?''

Arthur blinked. "Heraldic terms are simple once you

learn them…. Let me explain a little. The *crest,* this bit at the top, appears to be *lion statant.* That's a lion standing on all fours. He's above what I think is a ducal coronet—''

"This is a duke's coat of arms, Arthur?" Julia interjected.

"It would have to be. Then underneath the coronet a helmet, and under that we have the *arms*—in this case a shield divided quite clearly into four sections, or *quarterly.* See there? On each side of the arms are the *supporters,* which are these animals you see standing on their hind legs. One, as you see—'' He held the ring and the magnifying glass at an angle for the other two to peer through. "The one on the left—*sinister,* from the Latin—seems, by its horns, to be a stag. The other is less clear. Now all we have to do is narrow our search to those coats of arms that include these items. With luck there will be only one.''

It was an hour before they were certain. Arthur spread the book open at the page, and Julia and Rashid gazed down at the brightly painted coat of arms of the Worthingtons, Dukes of Rochester.

On the facing page was the description.

Arms: quarterly, first and fourth, azure, three bars ermine with a border engrailed or. Second and third, sable, a chevron or.

Crest: a lion statant guardant or, engorged with a ducal coronet sable.

Supporters: dexter, a talbot argent; sinister, a stag argent, gorged with a collar as the crest.

"Teneo quod teneo.''

His Grace the Most Noble Richard Fitzroy Charles Robert Worthington, Duke of Rochester, Baron Spellbridge, Baron George of Halstead, Knight of the Most Noble Order of the Garter, Companion of the Most Honourable Order of the Bath, Grand Steward of the Forest of Mere.

"What does the Latin mean?" Rashid asked.

"'I hold what I hold,'" Arthur supplied, with a sigh for the glory days.

"There's a short history of the title here," Julia said, her eyes running down the page. "'First Baron Spellbridge, Sir Fitzroy Worthington, 1426; first Earl Worthington, 1679; first Duke, 1713.'

"I'm as mystified as ever." She turned to Rashid. "Does your family have any connection with English aristocracy?"

"In 1890?" He shrugged. "It was a long time ago, and plenty of aristocratic Englishmen toured Tamir in the days of the British Empire." He turned to Arthur. "This book only takes us up to 1850. Who was the duke in 1890?"

Arthur patted the smaller, neater book. "This was published in 1940. Now that we have our man, let's look for him in here." He flipped through the modern book and stopped at the page where a smaller version of the same coat of arms sat over a lengthy printed history. "Ah," he said. "The title has been extinct since 1892, when the ninth duke died without issue."

Julia snapped her fingers. "Wait a minute! Delia made friends at school with a girl whose father was a duke! Why not start there?"

She turned to Arthur. "I'd like to look at the family correspondence for 1891 and 1892 again, Arthur. There must be a mention somewhere in her letters of Lady Elizabeth's family name."

When the archivist returned, he carried the several large

file boxes she had glanced through before. He placed them on the table. "These contain the personal correspondence of 1891 and 1892, including letters to and from Delia, Ugo and Julius while they were in England," he said, shifting the top two boxes. "And these are the estate and business letters for those years, and the big binder is for the letters of state. The family was meticulous about preserving correspondence, a habit that must have been bred into each succeeding generation. But sadly they were not always careful in dating letters."

"Now it's all on computer." Julia smiled.

Arthur sighed the sigh of a man outliving his time, lovingly patted the stack, and went away.

Julia carefully pulled on the fine white gloves Arthur had supplied to prevent their sweat damaging the old papers, dragged a box labelled "1890-95 Family Correspondence" down in front of her and opened it on a mass of letters. She flipped them over carefully, looking for Delia's distinctive paper, which she had learned to recognize during her previous foray into this box.

Meanwhile, Rashid took the binder marked "Letters of State 1890-93" and began to browse through.

"She was terribly homesick," Julia said after a few minutes, having separated out a small clutch of letters Delia had written home from the school in England. She squinted at them, trying to make out the often difficult writing. "And she was freezing to death in London. She'd never experienced a real winter before, I imagine. *Every room has what they call draughts. A draught is an ice-cold wind that seems to come from northern—*" Julia paused, frowning. "Northern what?…oh! Nowhere! …*that seems to come from nowhere to rush around one's ankles and strike into the heart.* That was in January, 1891."

"I feel for her," said Rashid with a grin. "To go straight

from Montebello to the middle of an English winter must
have been a shock.''

"Halstead House," Julia remarked, her eyes falling on a
sheet of white, headed paper covered with Delia's handwriting. "She must have gone on a visit to someone's...oh!
Listen. *His Grace is a fine-looking man, with fair hair and
sparkling*—no, not sparkling, what is this word? Speaking!—*and speaking blue eyes. Everyone agrees how well
he fills his noble position.*"

Rashid leaned back and rubbed his jaw, listening.

*He was very gracious to me, and said it was an honour
to welcome the Princess of Montebello, though I could
plainly see that some of his other guests thought it a
much greater thing to be Duke of Rochester than Princess of Montebello! I hope what I say does not pain
my dearest Papa. The English are very proud, I have
learned. That is what makes His Grace's kindness to
me so particularly remarkable. Another young lady
guest is angry with me, but indeed, it is none of my
doing.*

"There he is!" Julia remarked. "The Duke of Rochester.
But was the duke her friend's father, or someone else?"
She frowned down at the paper. "*Thursday*, that's all it
gives for a date!''

"How long was she in England?" Rashid asked.

"I was always told she spent a year at the school. Then
she returned home for a visit before going back for her
coming-out.''

She picked up another delicate green sheet and crowed
with delight.

"This is the one! Dated February 18, 1891, a few weeks
after her arrival at the school.''

*Lady Elizabeth Worthington, whom I told you about
before, has been particularly generous. She spoke so
kindly to me yesterday, when I was missing my dearest
Papa and Mama very much. She was very interested
to hear about dear San Sebastian's long days of sunshine and warmth. In return she told me about her
own beloved home, Halstead House. She says the
grounds there are the loveliest in the kingdom. She
has promised to take me to her own dressmaker for
the purchase of a fur muff, which she says will make
me entirely comfortable. We are to be friends.*

Julia looked up. "So. There's the connection. Her friend
Elizabeth's father was the Duke of Rochester."

Rashid, on the opposite side of the table, looked up from
his binder with a pensive frown. "A connection, but no
logic. Why would her friend's father's coat of arms be on
Delia's engagement ring?"

"I wonder if it wasn't her engagement ring at all. Maybe
after her death it was sent to your family by mistake. Suppose the two girls exchanged rings? There must be more
than one pigeon's blood ruby that size in the world, and
who would be more likely to have one than a duke's daughter?"

"Trade her engagement ring?" Rashid demanded in disbelief.

Julia laughed. "You're right. I was forgetting."

"I hope you won't be so absentminded when you are
wearing my engagement ring!"

She couldn't meet his eyes, so she opted for bravado.
"As I will never be wearing your engagement ring, I think
I can safely promise never to trade it."

Rashid smiled. "I love to hear you tempt fate like this,
Julia. It gives me hope."

She turned back to the letters without a word, and for a while there was silence in the shadowed room, broken only by the flick of a page being turned.

The Duke is a great huntsman. When I told him how I fear for his safety when he is out, he only laughed at me. But I know there are terrible accidents sometimes. You will think your daughter foolish, but when they are out at the hunt I find I cannot settle to any occupation.

"Mmmm. A little extreme, don't you think? Do you think Delia was over-emotional?" Julia murmured, when she had read this out.

"Perhaps she had a natural partiality for older men."

"Well, if so, it didn't last. Unless—how old was Omar?"

Rashid shrugged. "A young man."

"Oh, listen to this!"

Lady Elizabeth tells me the house party is much subdued from what it has been in other years, because of the family still being in mourning. She is to make her come-out in the spring, a year delayed.

Julia flipped the page over and shook her head. "She doesn't seem to have dated anything that came from Halstead House! I wonder who they're in mourning for. The duke didn't die till the following year."

Rashid said suddenly, "Here are the letters between our two forebears on the subject of the engagement."

Julia jumped up and ran around to look over his shoulder. A large oblong paper covered in beautiful Arabic calligraphy was sealed with an intricately curlicued seal in red wax.

"What does it say?" she demanded.

"In very formal and oblique language it acknowledges King Augustus's embassy offering the possibility of closer diplomatic ties between the two countries and suggests that a marriage between the two families might be of advantage in sealing the new agreement."

There was a long moment of silence, which Julia found herself reluctant to break. "I wonder what our countries would now be to each other if this forward-looking approach had come to fruition," Rashid said. His thumb stroked the red sealing wax.

"My father still uses a seal like this. It is only a little more than a hundred years ago. Many wise initiatives take longer to be realized."

Shortly afterwards, they abandoned their work for the day. It was already sunset, and Julia and Rashid wandered in the gardens until dinnertime.

"Why are we doing this?" she asked. "Why do you want to re-examine this old, bitter wound?"

"Because the truth may be important. And we have discovered that we have two very different ideas of the truth of this feud."

"Maybe it would be better to leave things as they are."

"Julia, you've given me reasons why you won't marry me. One, that I'm a Kamal and you're a Sebastiani and the feud between us is an insuperable barrier. The second, that you do not want to marry for political reasons again. Have I got that right? That you do not love me."

She bent her head. *And you don't love me,* she finished to herself.

"In this life a wise man learns to recognize the things he can change. That you are a Sebastiani and I am a Kamal, I cannot change. But that our two families hate each other—that may be changed. It is this single dispute that lies between us, nothing else. Perhaps by finding the truth of that dispute, we can let it go.''

''We might make it worse,'' she protested.

He shook his head. ''What could be worse than an accusation of cold-blooded murder? If we prove the murder was committed by your forebears, at the very least you will have to grant that the accusation has not been unjustified. If something else comes to light, my father will have to give up his position and apologize for a century of wrong.''

Julia sighed. ''I'd like to unravel it, I guess,'' she admitted. ''It would be something just to know what really happened, wouldn't it? If we can. But it won't change my mind about marriage, Rashid.''

Overhead the stars were coming out. Rashid stopped and turned her to face him. ''I have told you, Julia. I intend to remove your objections, one by one. When you have no objections left, what then?''

''You can't remove all of them!''

''No?'' he said, with a smile deep behind his eyes. Her heart began to race. ''How many times did your father propose to your mother?''

Julia bit her lip and turned away. ''That has nothing to do with us!''

''How many times?''

''Five!'' she told him grumpily.

''And how many times have I proposed to you?''

''Two! And I hope you don't think—''

She stopped because he was laughing. ''Ah, Julia, you're counting! That is excellent!'' His hand came up to tilt her chin up till her eyes were forced to meet his.

''One by one,'' he repeated softly.

Chapter 12

"**Y**ou're investigating Prince Omar's death?" the king repeated with surprise.

"You see, Papa, the Kamals have a very different story of what happened than our version. And that naturally has contributed to the misunderstanding over the years."

King Marcus's face stiffened. "It doesn't surprise me in the least to learn that your family has an erroneous idea of what went on, Rashid, but I'd be amazed if our 'version' of events, as Julia calls it, wasn't correct."

Rashid nodded. "In which case, I hope to find a proof sufficient to convince my father. In my opinion, it is time we laid this feud to rest. It benefits no one."

"I doubt if unearthing proof of the facts will carry much weight with your father, Rashid. He's got a vested interest in sticking to his point of view."

"With respect, I think you underestimate my father. He will not ignore the written evidence that Princess Delia was not sent to London against her will, for example."

Julia could see that her father had a lot of respect for Rashid and was starting to like him—against his will.

"And where will all this get you?" he grunted.

"I hope it will get me married," Rashid told him calmly. "Julia will not marry me while she feels that to do so would be a betrayal of the family. It seems a better approach to try and do away with the source of that feeling rather than attempt to persuade her to overcome it."

Her mother and father were silent, gazing between Julia's flushed face and Rashid's calm one.

Anna was watching the prince, fascinated. He clearly had one fan at the table. "Do you think you'll be able to?"

He smiled. "I hope so."

"By doing away with the source of Julia's feelings, do you mean that you think you can convince your father to withdraw his claim for Delia's Land?" asked the king.

"That, among other things. If we find evidence that your grandfather Ugo and his brother, Julius, were involved in Omar's death, I would also hope that your resentment over the century-old accusation would cool."

"I won't be giving up the land, whatever you prove. It was always an outrageous claim, however Omar met his death."

"I take your word for how things are in your own tradition. In the Tamiri tradition, however, King Mukhtar's response was a very restrained one. My ancestor could have sought the deaths of Ugo and Julius as his revenge. Instead, he took the softer option, demanding, in effect, blood money. Many people at the time would have seen this as a sign of weak will. His reign might have been threatened."

Marcus blinked as this new idea struck him. "Really," he murmured after a moment.

"There is a letter from King Mukhtar in your archives, pointing this out to King Augustus, saying that blood money was the least demand he could make consistent with his own honour and pleading with Augustus to recognize the justice of his claim so that he could put the incident behind him. Unfortunately, the translation of this and other documents was substandard.''

Marcus seemed stunned to silence, and it was Gwendolyn who asked, ''Who translated it?''

Rashid leaned back in his chair and lifted a hand. Julia thought distantly what an attractive, masculine grace his movements had.

''By what I can see, an English 'Arabist' who was employed by Augustus, named Arnold Chowndes-Hartley. He was not as skilled as a man in his position needed to be. If the same man translated Augustus's replies to Mukhtar into Arabic, it is a wonder the two countries didn't come to all-out war. A properly skilled and learned man in that position might have defused the whole crisis.''

''Fascinating,'' Gwendolyn breathed. ''Of course one never thinks of someone so minor as a translator or interpreter having such a profound effect.''

''Chowndes-Hartley seems to have been well aware of his own deficiencies,'' Rashid said with a rueful grin. ''He kept no copy of the Arabic translations that were sent to Mukhtar, only the English originals. And he seems to have destroyed many of his translations into English of the Tamiri letters. No doubt to protect his reputation from future historians.''

''Do you mean that all we have in the archives are the Arabic originals of the Tamiri documents and the English drafts of the letters Augustus sent to Mukhtar?'' Anna demanded.

''That's about the size of it.''

''So we have no way of knowing what was really said!''

''I will check our archives at home when we have finished here," Rashid said. "If the documents still exist a comparison will be possible."

Marcus cleared his throat. "Well, you had better stay with us while you're engaged on the task here."

Rashid smiled and nodded his thanks. "And will you wish me luck with my mission, sir?"

"You'll need more than luck when it comes to convincing that father of yours," said the truculent king.

Later, Julia and Rashid went to the sitting room of her private apartments. Her mother had taken it for granted that Julia would prefer to have Rashid in a bedroom in her suite, and Julia had been too torn to argue. She did and she didn't want him there, and if she couldn't explain that to herself, how could she hope to explain it to her mother?

So Rashid was put into a bedroom leading off her sitting room, and no doubt everyone, including her parents, assumed he wouldn't be using it. Julia didn't know how she felt about that, either.

Nor did she know how Rashid felt about it. He had accepted these arrangements without comment, and as they moved into the softly lighted room, Julia was getting nervous. What had happened on Erimos had been a time out of time. Something separate from her daily life. She had been able to pretend she was not a Sebastiani, and Rashid not a Kamal.

But now they were right in the middle of her life. It wasn't possible here to make that pretence. Everything around her, from her favourite books to the ornaments brought back from foreign trips or given to her by visiting dignitaries, shouted out that she was Her Royal Highness Princess Julia Sebastiani.

"You are nervous of me," Rashid said, cutting into her thoughts. Julia started.

"Not...not really."

She walked over and stood looking out the window. It looked southeast, like her bedroom window—towards Tamir. Her nanny's voice sounded in her memory. *King Ahmed Kamal will come and get you if you're not a good girl! He'll come right across the water and fly in this window and he'll put his curse on you!*

"Julia, believe me, I understand."

She turned. He was still in the middle of the room, looking as if he owned it. It occurred to her that he was like a panther. He could be self-effacing, almost invisible, when it suited him. He could be gentle. But always, underneath, was the promise of power. She felt his tenderness like the touch of a large paw, and thought—*what happens when he's finished playing with his prey, and wants his lunch?*

"What do you understand?"

"That here in the palace we will not make love. That there is no 'time out of time' for us here. That you are someone else now."

Her breathing was suddenly audible in the silence. She swallowed and bent her head. "All right," she agreed.

"For me, too, it is better not. When you are here in the palace I see in your eyes how you think of me. Your enemy. It would not be right for our bodies to love independent of our spirits. I do not wish to sleep with my enemy."

"You did before," she said, not really understanding this.

"No. In the château I could believe that you considered the matter as I did. And even on Erimos, you were different. Not a Sebastiani, but a woman. Now it is otherwise. And perhaps I could seduce you, with touch and with kisses, to violate your conviction. But I do not want any more moments out of time with you, Julia. I want only—the prelude to a lifetime of sharing."

So he did use the bedroom he was given, after all.

London. Dear Julius, today we returned to school. We came in the Duke's carriage the whole way, because, as he says, once the carriage is out, it is as easy to take it the whole way into Town as to the train station, which is not close. What a delightful time I have had! I do not know when I have been so happy in this country before. I have met many pleasant people. It quite lowers me to think that perhaps I shall never see some of them again. Lady Elizabeth cheers us with the thought that the Duke is sure to visit when he comes to Town. I wish you could meet her. She is the most delightful girl.

Halstead. Dearest Mama and Papa, His Grace has offered to mount me for the hunt. He says he has a horse very suitable for a lady and will ride with me and see that I come to no harm. Lady Elizabeth encourages me, as she hunts herself and says there is no pleasure like it.

Halstead. Dearest Papa and Mama, The Duchess is a very kind woman. In the country Lady Elizabeth and I are to be treated almost as if we had come out. She says girls are best when they have had some practice in Society before being launched, and where better to get that practice than in the protection of their own home? There is another young lady in the party, the Honourable Olivia Downing, who is not pleased by the Duchess's arrangement. She had her come-out last year, and I am sure she feels she ought to have more right to the attentions of the company than I. Dear Lady Elizabeth has such grace no one would guess that she is not already out. But as I explained to you, mourning delayed it all for a year. She is to come out

in London in the spring, however, and will be pre-
sented to the Queen. How I would love to have a taste
of London society!

Halstead. Wednesday. Dear Julius, How kind the Duke
is! Last night at dinner I committed a dreadful error.
Lady Elizabeth told me afterwards that it is simply not
done here to speak across the table, and I must re-
member not to do so again. The young lady I spoke
to cut me in the most humiliating manner. But I was
near the top of the table, and the Duke immediately
spoke to me, saying, "I believe Miss Downing was
referring to the walnut grove on the far side of the
park, were you not, Miss Downing?" So that she had
to acknowledge me. I do think that His Grace is the
kindest, most generous man I have ever met, except
for Papa.

London, Tuesday, November 10. Dearest Papa and
Mama, It gives me the greatest delight to inform you
that Lady Elizabeth has received permission from her
parents to spend Christmas with us! How I long to see
you all, after nearly a year apart! You will think me
quite grown up, I daresay.

"I think we're getting there, slowly," Julia said, examining the dozens of Delia's letters she had spread out on
one of the library tables and shifting their positions vis-à-
vis each other from time to time. They were trying to es-
tablish a chronology for the letters, and were working under
the disadvantage that some were missing, only a few were
fully dated and in some the handwriting was difficult to
decipher.

"Let's see how this fits. Delia arrives in London at the

school in late January, 1891,'' she said. ''She meets Lady
Elizabeth Worthington. At Easter Delia is invited to Halstead
House, where she meets the duke and duchess. She and the
duke conceive an immediate fondness for each other.

''Through all this she writes her favourite brother, Julius,
a few letters, but mostly she is writing to her parents. At
some point brother Julius comes to London to join his
brother, Ugo, at Sandhurst. She continues to write him.

''Delia makes several more visits to Halstead House during the course of the year, the last apparently in November.
The duke seems to consider her under his protection. He
also visits the girls at their school and takes them out to
tea, but without the duchess. There are also a couple of
visits from Ugo and Julius, both at Sandhurst.''

Julia shuffled a few more letters as Rashid watched with
a smile.

''Late in the year, Delia asks permission to return the
favour by inviting Elizabeth to Montebello over the Christmas period. Elizabeth's mother was going to launch her
into society in the spring. The duchess invites Delia to be
launched along with her friend. Delia's practically flying
with delight. She begs her parents to allow it, and although
they are strangely reluctant, they do eventually give in. That
takes us almost up to the end of 1891. I think.''

She scooped those letters into one pile. ''Once back in
Montebello, Delia starts writing to Julius, who is still in
England, much more regularly.

''This must be the time when she first hears about her
engagement to Omar. So I think that next on the agenda
have to be the letters to Julius.''

They had set aside Delia's letters to Julius that were written from Montebello.

''So let's get started,'' she said, blowing out a breath.
They really needed an expert on nineteenth century hand-
writing, she felt. They were getting only half the picture.
At first they had taken turns trying to read them out, but

Julia had more success than Rashid, owing perhaps to the fact that English was her first language.

"*San Sebastian,*" she read. "*Dear Julius, How I wish you were at home this holiday! I know so well how you would like Lady Elizabeth if only you could meet!* Sounds as if she's trying for a bit of matchmaking, doesn't it?" Julia interjected. "*She is so lovely, with the same fair hair and blue eyes as her brother—* No, that must be mother," Julia corrected herself. *And she seems delighted with Montebello. Yesterday we went around the clifftop path on muleback....*"

"Why must it be mother?" Rashid asked.

"Because we know Elizabeth had no brother. The duke died in 1892 without issue, remember?"

Julia set the letter to one side. "Minute description of fun and frolic," she said.

San Sebastian. Dear Julius, My papa has just broken some very strange news to me. I wonder if you know it already. Crown Prince Omar of Tamir has asked for my hand in marriage. Or rather, his father the King has done so on his behalf. Papa and King Mukhtar believe that the marriage will create a bond between our two nations. Of course I must be obedient to my father's wishes, but it seems very strange that I shall be married to a stranger. Papa says I will go to Tamir to live in the palace, and that I will be glad to be Queen one day. But I am sure I never shall. I know I can write my heart to you, my dearest brother. I had so much rather not be a Queen.

Julia looked up. "There's a blotched bit here that looks suspiciously like a tear. Funny that she was so opposed to it at the beginning, isn't it?"

"Is it?" Rashid prompted.

"Well, you'd think she'd have some curiosity about her fiancé, wouldn't you? And some hope. Delia just flat knows she's not going to like it. No adventurousness at all. Yet she went off to England all on her own."

Rashid pursed his mouth. "Perhaps she was already in love?"

"Who with? She hasn't mentioned anyone in her letters. The only man she writes of with any fondness is Elizabeth's father. Anyway, she fell in love with Omar once she met him, didn't she? I wonder if she wrote her brother after that meeting?"

San Sebastian, 4 January, 1892.
Dearest Julius, Papa has agreed that I am to be allowed to go to London for my Season after all. The engagement is not to be made public till my return, though I am to meet with the prince in a fortnight. I am so thankful! Indeed, he is an excellent father and I must never think of paining him. We leave in three weeks....

"There, you see?" Julia broke off reading to crow. "No force was needed to get her to go to London—she was dying to go! Look, here's the tear blotch."

I am so happy I can hardly write. You will think this letter dreadfully blotched, but oh, Julius, it is with tears of happiness.

Julia looked up triumphantly. "Do you think we should take a copy of this letter to your father? Would that serve to convince him of anything?"

Rashid took the letter from her and examined it curiously. "Yes, I am hoping to make a file of evidence for him, and this certainly should be included. But we have not yet heard from her after her meeting with Omar. Perhaps she changed her mind."

Julia took this as a challenge. "All right, she says they're meeting in a fortnight. So let's look for a date around two weeks after this. She seems to be writing Julius every week at this time, so—"

San Sebastian, 15 January
Dear Julius,
I have met him. Prince Omar and his father sailed into San Sebastian harbour just in advance of a terrible storm at sea. I tremble to think what might have occurred if their ship had been caught in it. It was an official visit, with trumpets and parades.

You will wish to know how the prince strikes me. I tried to write "my future husband" but my hand failed. He is very dark, with black eyes, and a proud, noble face. Not as tall as…he is about your height, perhaps. I believe he would be called handsome, but I thought him very savage.

He gripped my hand hard and looked into my face in a way that frightened me. All the while thunder pounded overhead like cannon, and lightning illumined the proceedings. The prince gave me a ring and said that he hoped our marriage should take place very soon. He speaks English very indifferently.

I was hard pressed to understand him, and almost weeping from nervous excitement, but he did not relent. I repeated that it could not happen before my visit to England. Papa had already explained it all, I know, but His Royal Highness pretended to anger, declaring that it must and should happen at once, all the while clasping my hand till it hurt.

My heart misgives me. What will become of me in that strange, alien place, without my Papa and Mama, without you? Oh, Julius, how I wish things could be otherwise!

"Not a very promising beginning," Julia murmured. "I wonder how long it took her to change her mind."

Rashid frowned. "Do you think it possible?"

"That she went on to fall in love with him?" Julia shrugged. "We know she must have."

"I imagine her shrinking away from him, and that spurring his predatory instinct, so frightening her even more."

"You could say he's got it all, though," Julia objected. "Handsome, dark eyed, noble, and passionately in love with her."

"You think she liked dark eyes?"

"Well, her description sounds like the prince in a fairy tale, doesn't he?"

"Does he?"

Julia shrugged. "That's how I always saw him, anyway—curling black hair and black eyes, and looking as if he could see off the evil magician or the wicked knight with one flick of his glimmering blade."

Rashid laughed a little. "She was steeped in a culture that was very English. And I am sure Omar was all Arab."

"I still think she could have fallen in love with him in the end," she argued. "Her letter doesn't accuse him of anything really sinister. Just passion."

"Julia, she practically admits she wishes the ship had sunk in the storm."

"People do fall in love after initial hostility, though, don't they?"

Rashid smiled at her with approval bright in his eyes, and Julia blushed and suddenly felt she'd been had. "We're talking about *Delia*," she said.

"Yes," he agreed. "But all the same I am glad that the prince you saw when you read your fairy tales had dark hair and dark eyes."

Chapter 13

Neither of them could afford to take time off from their duties forever, and that night Julia had to attend an Arts Gala.

"Shall I come with you?" Rashid asked.

Julia laughed. What a fluttering *that* would cause! "It's a media event," she said. "It's the kickoff to the San Sebastian film festival. We'd make waves, appearing together. Especially after I've just denied that we're engaged."

Rashid shrugged. "What do we care for that?"

Julia suddenly realized she'd prefer to have an escort—especially the dark and dangerous-looking Rashid. *At least I bet they won't print any more snide suggestions that I'm frigid, with Rashid staring at me the way he does,* she told herself.

Rashid flew home late that afternoon and returned looking extremely handsome in black tie. Julia, meanwhile, had changed into a beautiful ice-blue ball gown with a low scalloped neckline. It was split thigh high on one leg. Snug across her abdomen, it made no attempt to hide her pregnancy. She wore her hair piled up around her diamond tiara in a casual disarray that had taken Micheline an hour to achieve. For jewellery she wore her "lucky" bracelet, and a diamond necklace and earrings.

"Let them *dare* to call me the Ice Maiden!" she joked.

"No one who looked into your eyes could do that, even if your dress were made of diamonds. They are more likely to call you the Fire Witch. You are very beautiful tonight, Julia," he went on, in a warm, seductive voice that turned her skin to liquid honey and reminded her that last night they had slept in separate bedrooms. She bit her lip and turned away.

The gala was held in San Sebastian's beautiful old theatre, which dated from Victorian days and had been converted into a cinema in the sixties. There were film celebrities from all over the world in attendance, but the organizer nearly fell over backwards when he saw who Julia's escort was.

"Your Royal Highness, what a very, very great pleasure!" he said, as his assistant executed a tortured curtsey, whirled on her heel and disappeared up the steps and into the theatre at a dead run, obviously bound on some errand occasioned by Rashid's appearance.

"They're hotter than Charles and Camilla," Julia overheard an enthusiastic voice exclaim as they mingled with the other invitees in the magnificently restored Victorian lobby. "Who would think she'd turn up with him after that interview she gave?"

"Woman can always change her mind," quipped a dry male voice.

Julia couldn't help the little glance she tossed Rashid's way. He met it, his eyes alight with humour, and she suddenly remembered how starved for such companionship she had been when married to Luigi. They had never shared a sense of humour. She had been alone all through her marriage, and in that moment a treacherous voice whispered that perhaps a political marriage with Rashid would be significantly different than what she had suffered through with Luigi.

Of course he wants you to think so, another voice replied. *It's all part of his peace campaign, to convince you that together you could make it work.*

But even so, she enjoyed the gala more than any event she had attended for years.

Julia Will Marry Me!

Julia and Crown Prince Rashid Kamal of Tamir are "destined for each other" and will inevitably marry, according to Rashid. The prince, making a surprise appearance at the opening gala of the San Sebastian Film Festival last night, insisted that Julia was merely exercising her right to be "thoroughly wooed" before capitulating. To the obvious surprise of event organizers, the royal couple arrived at the gala together and stayed close throughout the evening.

"What the *hell* do you think you're doing?" Julia demanded furiously. She was sitting at breakfast alone on the terrace overlooking the Rose Garden. She had nearly choked on her toast when the *Messenger* was brought to her, and instantly demanded the phone.

Rashid had returned to Tamir last night after the gala. *And how surprised I am to discover that he feels no qualms about flying the helicopter at night,* she had told herself, fuelling her indignation, while she was waiting for her call to be put through to him.

She didn't like to think that she had missed his presence in her apartments after he had gone.

"Fighting fire with fire?" Rashid said, in lazy reply.

"You have no right to do this!"

"Sure I do," he told her without heat. And before she could answer, added, "All's fair in love and war, remember?"

Julia gritted her teeth. "This is not love, remember?"

"So you say."

"But it'll damn soon be war if you keep this up!"

"Okay. I'll try to arrive tomorrow in time for the opening salvo."

"Arrive tomorrow?" Julia repeated stupidly.

"I'm here clearing my schedule of all but essential items for the rest of the week. I've already got people working on the archives here. But your archives naturally have the most potential. So I'll see you for breakfast tomorrow."

"You—"

"How do you feel about a day out on Erimos again?"

"What?"

"I was hoping for some more of that *time out of time*. I find I like it better than ordinary time."

"I have no intention of going to Erimos again!"

"You refuse to come with me to Erimos?" Rashid asked sadly.

"Yes, I do," Julia said, much more firmly than she felt. Memories of Erimos filled her with longing on more than one level. Funny how one little word could overwhelm her with the intoxication of freedom, and the memory of passion.

"All right," he said, capitulating. "I am very sorry, Julia. But I won't try to persuade you."

"Good."

"I may have to kidnap you again, of course," he joked, before she put down the phone.

She knew she had made the right choice. But—

O Romeo, Romeo!...Deny thy father and refuse thy name....

14 Rajab, 1309
From Omar ibn Mukhtar ibn Wasim al Sadiq al Kamal to his honoured father, King Mukhtar ibn Wasim al Sadiq al Kamal
In the name of The One God, The Compassionate, The Merciful
Peace and Blessings Upon You!
Honoured father,
God be praised, I arrived safely after a difficult voyage. It is wet and cold, and snow is indeed a remarkable phenomenon, as Ibn Batuti has recorded. But even stranger is the fog. Imagine that the air thickens into cloud all around your face, and that cloud is yellow and choking. But it is cold and there is no sand in it. Prayer has been difficult. I have purchased a small compass so that I may find East even when the day seems like night. The countryside is richly green and fertile, though they tell me that this is winter, and little grows at this season....

"Is 14 Rajab the date in the Islamic calendar?" asked Julia.

Rashid nodded. "We'll have to check how it corresponded to the Western calendar that year."

18 Rajab
...the Lady Delia is not at present in the capital, but at the home of the Duke of Rochester, about 15 miles

*by road. I have purchased horses and vehicle and in-
tend to call upon her. As we heard, it was this same
Duke who visited King Augustus in Montebello in the
week before the departure of Princess Delia from her
father's house and brought her back to this country....*

"The duke in Montebello?" Julia exclaimed. "What's
he talking about?"
"Perhaps the duke and duchess made a visit while their
daughter was there."

10 Sha'ban, 1309
*...the Princess's two brothers paid a call on me this
morning at the London hotel. They said their mission
was to explain that the Princess no longer wished for
the marriage. They asked me "as a gentleman" to
withdraw my claim.... I threw one of them down the
stairs of the hotel....*

Julia sat silent, envisioning that scene. "Is this his last
letter?"
"The last. The next communication is the telegram
informing the king of his son's death."
She couldn't help thinking of Lucas, of her father's
reaction to the telephone call telling him the plane was
missing. What worse tragedy for a man like that than to
lose his firstborn son?
"I don't get it. Why were Delia's brothers sent on such
a delicate mission? If Augustus was having second thoughts
about giving away the land with the newly discovered copper deposits, why on earth didn't he do it through diplomatic channels? Why not send an embassy to King Mukhtar?"
Rashid shook his head. "And why say it was Delia's

doing?'' he pointed out. ''In that period, what a woman thought of the matter would have been largely irrelevant. Her father had given her away. Her fiancé wanted her. She was a piece of property and as such had been formally disposed of.''

''There's one obvious conclusion,'' Julia murmured thoughtfully.

''Yes,'' agreed Rashid. ''That it was, in fact, Delia who wanted out. Her brothers went to Omar on her behalf, hoping to find him open to persuasion.''

''But why? If she loved him, why did she want out? And if she didn't love him—why did she kill herself when he died?''

They couldn't find any letters from Delia to Julius written after the meeting with Omar. That in itself seemed suspicious.

''Do you think it means Julius afterwards suppressed those letters?'' Julia mused. ''He received all her letters in London, but only brought certain ones home when he returned…unless…''

Julia got up and went to find Arthur, who was on a ladder inspecting the contents of a high shelf. ''Arthur, is it possible that some of Delia's letters to Julius could have been put somewhere else? Among his official papers somehow?''

Dusting his hands, Arthur carefully descended. It occurred to Julia suddenly that Arthur was getting a little old to be climbing ladders like this. She thought, *Arthur's nearing retirement age!* It gave her a pang. Arthur had been in the library for as long as she could remember. He was an invaluable resource whenever anyone had a question about family or Montebello history. He had briefed her several times over the years.

"Arthur, we ought to get you an assistant," she suggested gently.

He nodded. "Yes, I've been meaning to mention it to your father for a year or so now. You'll want me to train someone before I go, and it'll take time to do that effectively."

"I'll mention it to Papa."

He nodded. "Now, about these letters?"

"There are no letters from Delia to Julius after the middle of January, 1892. We're wondering if maybe Julius had some cause to keep them out of his general cache of correspondence, so they didn't go into the family correspondence file after his death. Possible?"

He stood thoughtfully wiping his hands with a cloth, then laid it on his stepladder.

"Julius was Foreign Secretary for much of his brother Ugo's reign," he said. "It's possible some personal correspondence got mixed up in the Foreign Office files for the period. That would be, let me see—1912 to 1939, I believe. Julius resigned to let a younger man tackle the job when Montebello followed Britain into World War Two. That would have been October, 1939."

Julia smiled in admiration. "Arthur, you'll never be able to train anyone to replace you."

He bowed. "Thank you, Princess. But remember that I have had thirty years to learn on the job. You will have to have patience with my successor for a decade or two."

They laughed together. "I'll make a start on Julius's official papers this afternoon."

When she returned to their work space, Rashid asked, "Do you have appointments this afternoon?"

"No, I've had Valerie clear the next couple of days. Not that I have that much on at the moment, anyway. I've only slowly been getting back into the swing of things."

"I plan to go down to San Sebastian for lunch. Will you join me?"

She loved the city during the week of the film festival. There was always a buzz in the air. "There'll be lots of paparazzi," she warned.

"We'll find somewhere they are not allowed across the threshold," Rashid promised.

San Sebastian palace was high on a cliff overlooking the postcard-pretty harbour and yacht basin of the town. The high palace walls fenced off a jutting point, so that the boundary of the estate was edged with cliff face that dropped straight down into the sea.

They went out a side door and around to the garages. The driver of a small delivery van was just closing his vehicle doors. "Hold on," said Rashid, as the driver strolled around to the cab. "How do you feel about a couple of passengers?"

So a minute later Rashid and Julia, perched on the pull-down seat behind the bemused driver, were driven through the manned gate unseen. The van was ignored by the photographers standing vigil there, and, laughing like children skipping school, they were taken quickly down into the town.

The main boulevard, bordering San Sebastian Bay, was lined on one side with the elegant white structures of the colonial era and shaded with two rows of tall, slender cypress trees. On the other side were moored yachts and sailboats, whose rigging clanked and sang in the breeze.

They got out of the van in a side street and wandered down the narrow cobbled street towards the bay. The sun was bright and hot, but there was a cooling onshore breeze. Julia, in a calf-length blue print dress, was wearing a chic panama hat, cream with a blue band, and sunglasses. Rashid was also wearing a hat and sunglasses, but it would be only a matter of time before one of the numerous celebrity-hungry paparazzi roaming the streets noticed the pair.

But for the moment they were invisible. They wandered through the lively street market where fruit and vegetables were being sold alongside beautiful craft work, children's clothing and movie videos, and then along the wooden pier amongst the smaller moored boats, admiring the smooth lines and teak decking. Out in the bay the larger yachts were moored, and their tenders zipped back and forth across the bay with supplies and people.

Julia always enjoyed times like this, her ''invisible'' moments when people in the streets either didn't recognize her or left her alone if they did, allowing her to be anonymous. But today was especially pleasant. She didn't want to ask herself why.

''Got any favourite places to eat?'' Rashid asked.

''I usually eat at my club,'' she said. But she didn't particularly want to meet friends or people she knew now.

''How about this?'' said Rashid, stopping beside a chalked sandwich board sitting on the pier beside a moored tender. *The Seafarer Restaurant. Lunch aboard a luxury yacht in San Sebastian Bay with a view of the cliffs,* the sign read.

''Like to try it?'' Rashid glanced around.

''Oh, it must be new. I've never seen this be—'' Julia began.

''If we're quick we might not be spotted,'' Rashid said, and arbitrarily handed her down into the small launch, as a sleepy driver awoke and started his engine.

''They don't seem to be doing a roaring trade,'' Julia commented, as they were piloted neatly past the moored boats and out into the bay. ''We're the only two customers.''

Rashid shrugged. "We can always change our minds if we don't like the menu."

Their tender soon arrived at an immaculate navy-hulled motor yacht, and Rashid leapt onto the landing platform and then handed Julia out. She went first up the ladder and was met at the top by a dark-skinned waiter in a pristine white jacket. He was smiling broadly, and Julia began to suspect that they were the first takers the restaurant had had today.

Well, if first impressions were anything to go by, the place would soon be a success. There was plenty of money in San Sebastian, so even if the menu cost the earth, they'd do fine.

"Welcome, Your Royal Highness," the waiter said, bowing and smiling broadly. *"Ahlan wa sahlan wa marhaba!"*

"Thank you," she said automatically, while a little ripple of foreboding travelled over her skin. She turned to Rashid. "Looks like our cover's blown."

"It was bound to be once we got aboard," he said blandly. He put his arm around her waist and they followed the waiter onto a fabulously appointed aft deck shaded by a navy-and-white-striped canopy. Julia stood for a moment looking around. It was a lot more luxurious than any floating restaurant she had ever seen. It was more along the lines of the yachts her friends' parents ran.

She sat down in a designer deck chair, put her feet up and accepted a spritzer from the drinks waiter. Another man approached and bowed, then said something in Arabic. She left it to Rashid to order the meal.

Rashid flung himself down onto a sofa beside her. Julia sighed. "It's so peaceful." Beyond the railing the whole of San Sebastian was spread out around the curving bay, the long avenue of deep green cypresses against the low white buildings beyond, and the town rising on successive levels behind, like a Greek amphitheatre. On the cliffs to the left, just visible, was the palace. Low on the right was the yacht club building, and beside it the street market they had just left.

Rashid and Julia chatted as they drank, she pointing out to him various landmarks in the town. The theatre where they had attended the gala was halfway up the encircling hill. The San Simeon Hotel, San Sebastian's luxury hotel for the rich and famous, where most of the celebrities who had come for the film festival would be staying, was on the far right, at the eastern tip of the bay.

Julia got to her feet to follow Rashid and the waiter to their table. There still didn't seem to be other patrons aboard, she saw, as they moved into the air-conditioned dining room. They were seated at a table for two laid with spectacular silverware and crystal, navy linen tablecloth and white linen napkins. A long table behind them, laid for eight, remained empty.

When their starters were served she tasted her rocket and Parmesan salad and then sighed. "Perfect," she breathed. "I'm really surprised the word hasn't got around about this place. I'd have expected half our film festival celebs to be on board. They usually go for the luxury places."

She barely heard the distant clang of the sea ladder being stowed, the subdued thunder of powerful engines starting up. A slow clanking told her the anchor was coming up. They were such ordinary sounds that Julia scarcely noticed.

When the waiter had gone, she leaned over the table a little and said, "I've been thinking. I've got a new idea."

Rashid's pupils expanded as he looked at her. "You've changed your mind?"

Julia blinked. "What? Oh! No, not about us. I'm talking about Delia."

"Pity," he said with a slow smile.

"Our big problem is, if she didn't love Omar, why did she kill herself when he died, right?"

"Our big problem is convincing you—"

"Rashid, could you be serious for a moment?"

"Julia, I am very serious."

He was looking at her in a way that made her heart thump in spite of her determination to be unmoved. She pressed her lips together and shook her head.

"You're making it very hard to stay on topic!"

"Good," said Rashid.

"Will you listen for a moment?"

"For much more than a moment. Tell me."

"I thought—Omar chased her all the way to England, right? Terrified that she was going to escape from the marriage, probably."

"Undoubtedly."

"Well, here's my idea—maybe Omar got Delia alone and raped her. And she sent for her brothers and told them the story. They visit him in London to challenge him about it. They have a fight and one of the brothers ends up being thrown downstairs. Omar's afraid the news will get back to his father so he writes him a letter giving him a completely false story. Ugo and Julius follow him next time he goes out, or lie in wait for him on a country road and kill him. Delia, meanwhile, feeling she's been ruined, maybe even fearing she's pregnant, kills herself."

Julia took another mouthful of her rocket salad, sat back and opened her eyes at him. "What do you think of that for a theory?"

Rashid took a mouthful of his own salad. He considered, nodding thoughtfully. "How does the redesigned engagement ring fit in to this theory?"

Julia shrugged. "You're right, that's the weak link. Unless she did it in a fit of grief after the rape. Trying to obliterate him without actually tossing away a very valuable ruby?''

"It's ingenious, Julia, but does it account for the Worthington coat of arms being on the ring?''

"Maybe Elizabeth gave her a diamond ring as a token of friendship and Delia decided to have the ruby set in the middle of it.''

Rashid's eyebrows went up. "Ah! That clicks! That would account for the strange setting—the ruby was put into a pre-existing setting. I wonder if that's possible. I'll take the ring to a jeweller for an expert opinion.''

"We need to check the dates of their two deaths, too,'' Julia said. "How long after Omar's body was found did Delia die? I wonder if Arthur can pull those dates out when we go back after lunch.''

Rashid's head was bent over his plate. He raised his eyes and looked at her with a look she couldn't read.

"Or perhaps we won't go back after lunch?''

She laughed involuntarily. "Not go back? Where would we go?''

"Anywhere you like. We could sail up to Erimos, or to Egypt....'' He shrugged. "Wherever.''

Julia drew in a soundless breath through her open mouth, and looked around. She should have known. Of course she should. She had been almost wilfully naive.

"This is your own yacht!'' she cried.

Chapter 14

Rashid smiled. "I did warn you that I would kidnap you again."

"Yes, you did, and what a fool I was not to realize you meant it! What do you think you're doing? You'll be lucky if we don't get the secret service dropping tear gas canisters on deck, or firing across your bow!"

"They will only become concerned if you activate an emergency signal, if your secret service is anything like ours."

She smiled grimly. "I ought to. Maybe it would teach you a lesson to have your shiny paintwork and fittings wrecked. They wouldn't be very gentle when it came to a kidnapping charge, I'm sure!"

"Why are you angry?" Rashid asked softly. "When you thought this yacht was a restaurant you were comfortable. Why does the fact that I own it change that?"

"Because you tricked me!"

"I have not tricked you very far. You know in your heart

that you are safe with me. You are not afraid. No harm will come to you here, and you know it."

Just then their main course arrived.

"Relax, Julia, and eat," he commanded. "Of course if you insist I will take you home immediately after the meal."

A charcoal-grilled tuna steak in a bed of salsa was set down in front of her, and her stomach tensed in anticipation.

"I can't imagine why you did it in the first place," Julia said, picking up her knife and fork and hoping this didn't look too much like capitulation.

"You know why," he said roughly, as if he had lost control of his voice abruptly. "I am hungry for more 'time out of time,' Julia. I want you in my bed."

Without warning a wave of heat rushed up her body. Julia cut a morsel of the tuna and put it into her mouth.

"What is your answer?" he demanded. He had not picked up knife or fork. His hands rested on the tablecloth on either side of his place setting.

"What's the question?"

He reached across the table to clasp her hand. Electricity came from his skin and from his dark eyes and pierced straight to her heart. "The question is, will you come to my bedroom with me this afternoon?"

She couldn't seem to swallow. "I thought you said that you didn't want to make love to me when I considered you an enemy."

"In the palace, when you look at me, there is something in your eyes that I do not like to see. Then you look at me from Sebastiani eyes, and you see a Kamal. Outside, it is not so. The look is not there now."

Julia's body twitched in surprise. "Really? There's a difference?"

"Here, Julia, you look at me the way a woman should look at the father of the child she carries within her. And you allow me to see you—the real Julia."

This made her acutely nervous. What did that mean, that he could see the real Julia? She was not aware of the change and was nervous about what he might think he saw.

"I want to go back after lunch," she said doggedly.

Rashid nodded once. He summoned the waiter and murmured something in Arabic, and after that they dropped the subject. Julia applied herself to the delicious meal. They talked about Delia through the main course.

"What would your father's reaction be if we proved that Omar had raped Delia?" she wanted to know.

"He would say that his death at her brothers' hands was justified," Rashid said matter-of-factly.

Julia breathed in a soft gasp. "Really?"

"Of course." Rashid lifted his hands. "How could it be argued otherwise? He would understand that her brothers wanted to protect her name but at the same time felt duty bound to avenge her. Only one course would have been open to them. Until 1967, there was a law in Tamir that allowed a family to seek private justice for such crimes. If we prove this against Omar, my father will renounce his claim to Delia's Land."

"I don't suppose we'll find real evidence, though."

"Unless Delia wrote of it to her brother in the missing letters," Rashid pointed out.

When they had eaten, they went out on deck again, where they were met with heat and the delicious silence of the Mediterranean, blue and tranquil all around them. An hour's sailing had taken them out of sight of any other boat. In the far distance a smokey pink shadow on the horizon was land.

"Would you like to see around the yacht?" he asked, and when she assented led her along the cedar deck past the windows of the dining room they had just left and back through a door into the adjoining saloon. There were stuffed armchairs and sofas around a couple of low tables, a bar with stools, a staircase running up to the next deck.

The decor was Middle Eastern, from the lamps to the Persian and Parvan carpets and the exotically woven furnishing fabrics. On one wall was a beautifully detailed mural like a Persian miniature. "It's a bit like a sultan's tent," Julia murmured, not sure whether she liked it. The Montebellan royal yacht, while luxurious, seemed subdued compared to this, being mostly done in beiges and creams.

He showed her the more formal dining room, and then along the passageway, from which doors on both sides led to guest rooms, to the master stateroom at the bow.

"Now, this really *is* a sultan's tent!" Julia cried, stopping on the threshold. Moroccan lanterns, Bagestani cushions and rugs, Parvani brassware, an unbelievably fabulous Persian silk-on-silk carpet, gold-embossed calligraphy on white leather framed in the Barakati style—all predominantly in shades of blue, ivory, tan and gold—together produced an impact of overwhelming, luxurious beauty.

It was the complete antithesis of Erimos, and she found herself curious about what it was in Rashid that allowed him to move with such apparent ease between the two worlds.

"It's stunning," Julia breathed, feeling as though she had entered another world, another time. She had never before experienced quite the ambience she felt on this yacht. *Nothing matters here,* the room seemed to whisper.

"Is this the Tamiri official yacht?" she asked.

"No, that is larger. This is my personal yacht, too small for official needs."

"What's her name?" Julia wondered. They had approached the yacht from aft, so she hadn't seen the name on the bow.

"Fitnah," he said. "Temptation, in English. Come."

He led her back down the passage and out onto the deck, so it hadn't been a trick to get her into the bedroom, she reflected. They went up a flight of steps to the bridge deck. There, behind the wheelhouse, was the sundeck, with a Jacuzzi and bar. Navy and white umbrellas were ruffling and flapping in the breeze above tables and chairs or loungers, and just the sound of the wind was pleasantly cool.

"Shall we have something to drink here?" Rashid asked.

Julia stood looking around on an expanse of wonderful blue. In the far distance she saw a lone white sail against the dark sea. Other than that they were alone with the Mediterranean.

"All right," she murmured. Rashid indicated two lounge chairs under an umbrella, half in sun, half in shade.

Julia sank down in the shade and kicked off her sandals, and when the waiter appeared, asked for sparkling mineral water.

"Bring us a bottle on ice, please," Rashid said. When their drinks and some snacks were set out on the tiny table that encircled the umbrella pole, they were left alone.

Rashid turned the other lounger around, placing it so that he was now facing her, their heads only a few feet apart. After a moment he lifted one dark strong hand and placed it on her abdomen. The weight of his sun-warmed hand was soothing, and she smiled.

"My son," he murmured. "You know that it is a boy?"

"I think it is. I could be wrong, I suppose."

"When did you know it was a boy?"

"Right from the moment I knew I was pregnant. I knew about that before any test could have proved it, too. Of course I hoped it wasn't true. Just a few days after…"

"After we made love at the château." Rashid filled the pause.

"I woke up in the middle of the night. I knew I was pregnant and that it was a boy."

"And that you would raise him without a father."

She sighed. "You were missing. It was possible that, like Lucas, you might not come back. It wasn't a decision I made, so much as realization of what the situation was."

"I am sorry necessity compelled what I did at that precise moment. If I had not had to leave… If I had been there when you woke in the night, you would not have had to face the necessity of raising your child alone. Perhaps I would have found it easier to convince you to let me share this with you."

She pursed her lips. He was right in one thing. Having to face her father with the facts on her own, feeling so alone, had somehow isolated her. She had drawn on reserves of self-sufficiency she didn't know she had. Maybe if that part of her had never kicked in, she would be less firm now.

"But you'd still be running against the wind, Rashid," she told him. "For the first year after Luigi and I split I promised myself I'd never marry again, no matter what. Then slowly I started to think, well, if I genuinely loved someone, and he loved me, it might be a possibility. But I'm a long way from thinking I could get married for the sake of peace between Montebello and Tamir. Or even to give my child a father.''

''And for the sake of making love with your husband on long hot afternoons at sea?''

The quick heat rose in her cheeks and she turned her head to one side, glad of the protection of her sunglasses. In the distance more boats were appearing. The yacht was getting closer to San Sebastian.

''Do you know how much I want you, Julia?'' He drew a ragged breath.

She closed her eyes and pressed her lips together.

''I dreamed of you after our night in the château, short as that was. How much more do you think I dream of you now? You are there in every dream, your body so beautiful, so open.... Do you know how your back arches to pleasure when my hand touches you? Your eyes squeeze tight, and those dark lashes cluster...and your mouth softens into a flower. Your hunger for the pleasure I can give you intoxicates me. I want to see that again. I want to hear those soft, seeking cries again. I want to taste the salt of your desire.

''And your body... I dream of you lying there, your legs spread for me. Do you remember that, Julia? Do you dream of my touch, do you dream of wanting me?''

She bit her lip against the cry that rose up in her. From behind her glasses she gazed into his dark, intent face and then away. In the distance now she could already see the forest of masts that marked the yacht basin.

''Your skin so smooth to my touch, your body coming alive...I see you at the water's edge, too, naked and dappled with sand, the water swirling under you, carrying your hair in patterns around your head. I see that in my dreams, Julia. In my dreams your hair turns into flower buds. I kiss each blossom the way I kissed your body, and the flowers unfurl for my mouth the way your body opened to me, and I feel you tremble with passion. Are you troubled by no dreams, Julia?''

She was alive with sensation and yearning.

"What do you want?" she pleaded.

"I want to know that you dream of me, that pleasure heats your body in your dreams. Do you dream of my hands, Julia? My mouth? Do you dream of my body hard for you, wanting to make you tremble?"

He was not touching her; he had lifted his hand away from her stomach, but the wind was enough. The wind and his voice, stroking her, so that her blood was a river of shivering sensation.

She bent one knee, sliding her foot along the hot fabric of the cushion. That touch, too, electrified her, and the breath hissed between her teeth.

She saw his jaw clench with the control he was exerting. "That sound drives me to the edge. I want to make love to you here, now, open to the sky, the way we made love on Erimos. And you, Julia—you don't yearn for this? It was enough, what we had? That little taste of lovemaking with me, that was all you wanted?"

She made no answer.

"Not for me," he growled. "If I make love to you every day and every night for eternity, still there will be something more to want from you. Is it not so for you, Julia? Do you think you have learned every secret of what my body can do for yours, in one day?"

She swallowed. "Rashid—"

"Yes, say my name. Tell me what you want. Tell me to turn this boat around and sail away with you. Tell me to take you down to my bed and give you more pleasure, and then more. Say it, Julia. Say it."

There was a shout in the distance, and then the thundering rattle of the great anchor chain as it was loosed to pierce the dark water. A deckhand came out of the wheelhouse and went past them down the stairs. More shouts, and the sounds of busy feet as the yacht was positioned and brought to rest.

They sat in silence, listening, till the engines died.

Arthur was waiting for her when she entered the library later that afternoon. His faded eyes were bright with interest.

"What is it?" Julia cried. "Have you found the letters, Arthur?"

"Not the letters." He led her to the table where she and Rashid had been working. There was another file box sitting there. The librarian patted it almost reverently.

"I wonder if the princess's diaries would hold any clues," he said.

There was a sudden, deep silence in the library. Arthur smiled as if he'd pulled a very fat rabbit from the hat.

"Delia's diaries?" Julia whispered at last.

"I've been on a trolling expedition since yesterday, to see what else there might be from the period. I found this cache this afternoon. Princess Delia kept a diary from the age of eleven to her death at age eighteen."

Eighteen! It seemed impossible she had been so young.

"Are they all there?" she choked.

"I think so. Her last diary was sent home from England with her other effects after her death. There is a note about it from John Dale, who was the archivist here after the First World War. During the twenties, he did a great deal of collating of the private royal papers. I thought I remembered reading a mention of the diaries in his log when I first took on the job."

He pushed the clip holding the box closed and pulled back the lid. Inside were maybe a dozen books, of differing shapes and sizes, from simple paperbound notebooks to volumes of tooled leather.

"Now we'll know the truth," Julia breathed. She realized only when she spoke that she was half afraid of the truth.

Monday, 5 January, 1885. Señor de Stephanis brought me this book for use as a diary, and I mean to be very good about keeping it. I am going to write in it every day. Mama says it is very useful to keep a diary, as it will encourage reflection and self-control....

Friday, 30 January. Ugo came in, very disturbed, to say that General Gordon is dead in Khartoum and the Mahdi has taken the city. On the 26th, the gates were opened to the rebels as the General slept. He was shot down in the street as he sought refuge. His head was afterwards paraded through the streets on a stick, to cheers from the populace. It is horrible. Why do men do such dreadful things in the name of war? Papa says...

Thursday, 18 June. Today I rode the new little mare Papa brought for me. She is very pretty and good-

*natured, a soft dun colour with black markings around
her eyes. I shall call her Bliss....*

*Wednesday, 4 November. Ugo and Julius have been
allowed to go aboard the British man o' war which
has docked in San Sebastian harbour....*

Julia turned the pages, her heart constricting with excitement and pity. This child, grave, thoughtful, quick to delight, had only a few years to live after these words were written.

"Princess?" Julia looked up from the stiff, crackling pages of the diary in a dream. "I'll be leaving now," said Arthur. "Would you prefer me not to lock up?"

"Oh!" she said blankly, as the world came back. "Oh, no, Arthur, you do what you normally do. I'll just take one or two of these volumes, if you think they'll be safe with me."

He smiled at the little joke, and Julia began flipping through the diaries in the box for the one she wanted. In the end she took two in addition to the very first one. One which was started fresh by Delia in January 1891 as she travelled to London to school, and the other which continued into 1892. Her last two diaries. Then she bid Arthur good-night and went up to her apartments.

When they had returned to the palace this afternoon, Rashid had said he had to get back to Tamir tonight and would see her in the morning. Then he'd gone across the lawn to his helicopter, and a moment later had lifted off.

At her window now, Julia gazed towards Tamir, invisible over the horizon, and tried not to feel disappointed. He had already told her he was clearing his schedule for a couple of days. He had urged her to sail away with him. She knew he didn't have to be in Tamir tonight.

He went because he didn't want to spend the night in her apartment. She was sure of that. Sure that he had known he would be tempted beyond his limits tonight. He was determined not to make love to her here. Not while she was so decided against marriage.

Her body was aching for him. He must have known that she could not say no tonight. That she would even have gone to him.

Her phone rang.

"Valerie, Princess. A reminder that your father is expecting you at dinner tonight."

"Oh, hell," Julia said mildly. "I was planning a nice quiet evening with the diaries."

"With the what?"

"Never mind. Who is it tonight?"

"I believe it's the British Ambassador and her husband."

It was late before she got back to her apartment, and even later before she got out of her formal clothes and makeup and could settle down with the diaries.

She had planned to start slowly, easing into Delia's life through the earliest diary, and then going chronologically through the last two. The first of these neatly covered Delia's year in England, including her arrival back in San Sebastian, just before Christmas 1891, with Lady Elizabeth.

But it was late, and suddenly she just wanted to know what had really happened to Delia. So she picked up the last of her diaries and took it to bed with her. There she plumped up her pillows, settled down, and opened the diary at the last few pages. She frowned at it.

5 March. Halstead. Wh ml 3 4t vl? Hwt ml 3 4t 4d? 6m rht lwl rbk. Brtr yss ht snrw s3 ys. 2h yss 3 smt rmyr mh. Htt 2w lwl ltl pp ht rtht…

Julia groaned with astonishment and vexation and desperately turned to an earlier page.

January 27, aboard the Queen of Montebello. Our journey has been a little rough, but no more than to be expected for this time of year. Lady Elizabeth is quite ill and keeps to her room. I never suffer from seasickness, and the Duke is similarly fortunate, so we are to keep each other company….

January 28. Queen of Montebello. Wh sdrthgt 3 ml. 6m rht lwl rbk n3 1 htsdn cps.

Julia sat up and flicked through the pages. At least half of the diary was indecipherable. Delia had written her secrets in code.

Chapter 15

"Codes and ciphers became very popular during the late Victorian period," Arthur told them next morning. "Partly it had to do with the spread of the telegraph. To send a telegram you had to expose your message to at least two strangers, or worse, to two people who were not strangers. The village postmistress, normally, I expect. If you look at the personal columns of *The Times* in those days, you'll find encryption of one sort or another was extensively used there."

"What sort of codes were used?" Rashid was peering down at an example of Delia's code. He had arrived early with a sheaf of photocopies from the Kamal royal archives, but had set them aside when Julia excitedly showed him the diaries.

"Two main kinds, I believe. A *cipher* is where one letter is substituted for another. Julius Caesar, for example, used a simple substitution cipher. *Code* technically means where words are substituted. The secret services probably use code to refer to each of you, for example. What do they call you, Princess?''

Julia smiled. "I think, Dancer." She turned to Rashid. "And they've changed yours just lately to Cupid."

"They have named me for the Greek god of love?" Rashid protested.

"Yes, and there's the added joke that they are the names of two of Santa's reindeer," Julia told him. "Anna is Prancer, and Christina was always Dasher. What do yours call us?"

"Just lately, I hear, you have become *Warda* and I am *Bulbul*. The *bulbul* is the Eastern nightingale, known for his hopeless unrequited passion for *al warda*. The Rose."

There was a small, pregnant silence, and then Arthur went on brightly, "Well, those are simple examples of code. But there are many other ways of encrypting messages. Delia appears to have used numbers as well as letters. I don't know what to make of that. Some ciphers are based on a keyword, and unless you discover the keyword you have little hope of cracking the code. You may need a cryptanalyst.

"Here's one example of the way a keyword cipher works." He opened a reference book on the subject and pointed to a series of letter squares. "You write your keyword, you see, and then underneath that you list the alphabet, and that gets written out column by column...."

They followed the method through. "It certainly looks complicated," Julia murmured sadly, with the sudden conviction that they could never crack Delia's code. "How would we ever find her keyword?"

"I wonder if she would have written it down for easy reference?" Rashid mused. He picked up the last diary again and flipped to the front. There was nothing on the flyleaf but the name Delia Sebastiani, and the figure 2/6.

"The price," Arthur supplied. "The diary presumably cost two shillings and sixpence. Half a crown."

After a last entry on March 14, the day before Omar's death and five days before Delia's own, the diary was nothing but blank pages. Rashid flipped through to the back.

Rashid bent over it in sudden alertness. "This isn't the original end paper," he murmured. "It is the back flyleaf of the diary glued down."

Julia and the librarian gasped in surprise. "Let me look!" cried Julia.

He was right. The flyleaf of the diary had been glued to the inside of the back cover. "Do you think she wrote her keyword on the end paper and then glued this page down to hide it?" Julia cried.

Arthur frowned. "But would she have had ready access to it, in that case?"

She was instantly deflated. "Oh, no, you're right! What would be the point? Still—"

Rashid was concentrating on the diary. "The stuffing of the cover has been tampered with," he said softly, pinching the leather-bound cover gently. "Here, feel it."

The diary was typical of many leather-bound volumes. The basic cover was heavy cardboard, with a tooled leather binding. Between the leather and the cardboard was some kind of soft cushioning material. As Julia squeezed the front and back covers, it was obvious that the back cover had been altered in some way. The stiff cardboard gave a little, and the stuffing was harder than at the front.

"We need to lift up that end paper," she said, her voice cracking with excitement. "But we have to be careful in case something is written there."

"Steam, I think," said Arthur. The three of them trooped to the little room which served as Arthur's kitchen-cum-workroom.

"I do the less complicated repairs myself," he explained

eagerly, as he filled the kettle and plugged it in. "If a book needs a complete rebinding job, of course we send that out."

For several minutes he carefully held the inside back of the diary over the steaming kettle, trying at intervals to lift the paper, before their efforts achieved results. Arthur carried the book to his worktable and flicked on the bright working lamp there.

What followed was like something out of a girls' detective story. The three amateur detectives crouched over the diary, hardly breathing. In complete silence, Arthur picked up a tool and carefully eased the glued sheet away from the inside cover.

A single sigh went through them. What was exposed was a neat oblong cut into the cardboard cover, which had clearly been lifted out and replaced. Arthur picked up another tool, and gently pried the oblong out of its frame.

As it lifted away, a folded paper came into view. "Delia's codes!" Julia breathed.

It was stained with smears of brown, and she felt Rashid stiffen into alertness. "I don't think so," he muttered.

Using a delicate pair of tweezers, Arthur prised the paper out and set it on his work top. Then, laying the diary to one side, he drew the paper under the lamp's beam and tenderly, slowly, so as not to cause the century-old document to crack, began to unfold it.

It was not the codes. It was a badly stained Special Licence of Marriage, issued by the office of the Archbishop of Canterbury, permitting the marriage of Robert Worthington, Duke of Rochester, and Delia Isabella Sebastiani.

"Ah, here we have it," said Arthur. "The *eighth* Duke, Robert, died in 1890, leaving the title and estates to his son, also called Robert."

They were sitting back at their regular table in the library, with assorted reference books around them.

"And it was the younger Robert, the *ninth* Duke, who died 1892, without issue, making the title extinct."

"Oh!" Julia cried sadly, having forgotten that part of the history.

"Do you have the exact date of his death?" Rashid asked.

"Not in this reference, I'm afraid. I'm not sure where such information could be obtained. Other than the Family Records Centre in London, where the records of births, marriages and deaths are held. Perhaps in the Worthington family archives, if they still exist. There's no mention here of what happened to the estate, of course."

"Or how he died?"

Arthur sat up. "Now, that sort of information will be—" He reached out for another large reference work and bent to consult it.

"The title became extinct when the ninth duke was killed in a tragic hunting accident in his twenty-sixth year of life," he read.

Rashid picked up the marriage licence and looked at it with one eyebrow raised. "I wonder if the Duke of Rochester was carrying his marriage licence while out hunting," he murmured dryly. "These stains are blood."

"It all makes sense now," Julia recapitulated. "Halstead House subdued and in mourning when Delia visited—it was for Elizabeth's *father!* And the duke who was so handsome and noble and with whom Delia shared an instant liking, and who came and took them to tea…that was Elizabeth's brother. The new duke! No wonder they were all talking about how nobly he fitted the role, with him only in his twenties!''

She gazed at Rashid with new respect. "You were right. Delia wasn't excited by the proposal from Omar because she was already in love. With the new young Duke of Rochester.''

For the next half hour they sat going over all the London and Halstead letters, reading them from this new vantage point, and watching Delia and her friend's brother fall in love.

"This is why she was so desperate to go back to London. Not just for the society launch, but out of some deep hope that something could be done to stop her marriage to Omar,'' Julia mused. "Or perhaps as a last moment of happiness before her fate was sealed.''

From the Commissioner of the Metropolitan Police
Colonel Sir Edward Bradford, Bt. GCB. GCVO. KCSI
28th September, 1892

To His Majesty King Mukhtar ibn Wasim al Sadiq al
Kamal
The Royal Court
Tamir

Dear Sir,
Further to our prolonged correspondence and your
most recent letter of the 5th inst, I can only repeat
what I have outlined to you on previous occasions.
The Metropolitan Police have investigated your alle-
gations against Prince Ugo Sebastiani and Prince Ju-
lius Sebastiani and have found no grounds whatever
to substantiate any suspicion that either or both are
implicated in the tragic death of your son. As I have
been at pains to make clear, the commanding officer

in charge of the young princes at the Royal Military College at Sandhurst, a gentleman and an officer of unimpeachable integrity, has testified that these young officers were on a field exercise throughout the period of 14 and 15 March, many miles distant from the scene of the crime, that he saw each of them numerous times during the course of both days....

"Seems pretty conclusive," Julia said.

"Yes," said Rashid. "I had no idea the investigations at the time had been so thorough. It's a pity Mukhtar didn't accept the evidence, but there are several letters that make it clear he thought it was a cover-up."

Julia leaned back in her chair. "And where do we go from here?"

"England," Rashid said. "To try and track down the Worthington family records if they still exist. I have business there anyway. I can put my trip forward. Will you come with me?"

Julia sighed thoughtfully. "I need to think about that. When would you go?"

"Tomorrow, I think, as I've already cleared my schedule."

"Let me think about it."

She took Rashid up to the Long Gallery, where the family portraits hung, and showed him a framed photograph of the doomed princess. He saw a slender girl of about sixteen, with a long oval face, her skin clear and luminous, her eyes grave. Dark hair hung down her back almost to her waist. A large white bow at the back of her head, a white dress covering the new young bosom.

She had the delicate nose of the Sebastiani women, the curving eyebrows. Her eyes held a longing that disturbed him at a deep level. She had a mouth like Julia's, full and with the promise of a passionate nature.

"I think this was taken just before she left for school in England. You can see she's just on the edge of womanhood, can't you?" Julia murmured. "I imagine that during the year in England she matured a lot."

"She would have become a beautiful woman," Rashid said. He felt moved by the face, perhaps because he knew what she had not known—that she would not live to fulfill her promise. That tragedy awaited her.

"And they both wanted her," Julia said.

"Yes. I am not surprised that Omar fell in love with her on sight. She is a woman you decide at once must be yours."

"Is she?" Julia breathed, biting back the urge to demand, *What kind of woman am I?* "I wonder if the duke fell in love at first sight, too."

"He was certainly in love with her before she returned to Montebello. That is why he came out to Montebello to escort her back to England."

"Think so?"

He looked at her. "He was determined that she would return to him, can't you see it? Of course he was worried that another man would see her and try to win her while she was at home."

She wondered how Rashid would respond to the threat of another man wanting her. Would he take it personally, or merely feel that his plans for peace were threatened?

"Yes, I see. I wonder if he'd declared himself before she left London. Do you suppose they were secretly engaged?"

"Wouldn't she have told her father about it when he raised the issue of Omar's proposal?"

"Maybe," Julia mused. "She might have been too

frightened. Or too dutiful. Duty was a high art then. Especially duty to the family.''

Rashid laughed aloud. ''And it isn't today?'' His laughter echoed down the gallery, making the windows ring. The painted faces of her ancestors seemed to stiffen.

''What do you mean?''

''Isn't it a sense of duty to your family that prevents you marrying me?''

Julia gasped. ''No!'' Then, ''What are you talking about?''

He shook his head patiently. ''What does your 'time out of time' mean, Julia? Doesn't it mean a time when you are not a Sebastiani and I am not a Kamal? And what does that say? You are making a sacrifice—how great only you know—on the altar of family duty.''

''That's ridiculous!'' she snapped.

He lifted his arm and waved at the long row of Sebastiani faces. ''Do they rise up in your dreams and tell you to keep away from me?''

''No, they do not!''

Rashid smiled. ''Good. Try and remember that in terms of family time, the feud that separates us is very recent. Your family governed in Montebello under the British Empire for several hundred years, did it not?''

''Since 1774,'' she said.

''So more than half of these men and women did not hate the Kamals. As for my family—we were governors under the Caliph Haroun al Rashid, first appointed in the year 803. What is a hundred and ten years measured against such a span of time?''

''I don't—''

He held her shoulders, touched her lips with a finger. ''A mistake was made, Julia. Together we are going to find out exactly what that mistake was. Then we will put it right, and history will resume its proper course."

"By me marrying you, I suppose!" she snapped, because she was moved by his words and wished she were not.

He smiled deep into her eyes.

"Yes," he said. "By you marrying me. Julia, we now know that whatever we uncover will prove that my family's suspicions about your family were wrong. This death can no longer stand between our two families once we have completed our work. I told you that I would work to remove your objections to our marriage. This is the first. Will you accept the others on trust?

"Will you marry me, Julia, and let me be a father to our son, and help me rule over a nation at peace?"

Julia closed her eyes. Perhaps if he had not pressed the claims of the baby and the country, she might have weakened. Or if she had never experienced what a marriage for the sake of politics was like.

"I can't," she whispered. "I can't."

Rashid sighed and gazed down at her averted face, but she couldn't look at him. Standing on the black-and-white-tiled floor in the dramatic light and shadow of the Long Gallery, they seemed like an Old Master themselves. *Portrait of a suitor wooing a woman already pregnant.*

That evening, after Rashid left, Julia went for a long walk down to the cliffs, and stood there, watching the sea. There was a stiff breeze and the surf was rough, pounding into the rocks underneath her.

There, watching the sun sink in a peaceful storm of red, purple and pink, she finally faced what had been staring her in the face for a long time: she was in love with Rashid. That was why she could not accept a political marriage with him. She thought of how humiliated she had been by

Luigi's rejection of her. That had been a purely sexual rejection, but it had been crippling. As a result she had become someone not herself.

It would be so much worse to be rejected from the heart. She didn't know how she knew that, but she was convinced of it. To love someone who didn't love you was bad enough. To marry that person, to spend your days waiting and hoping for some expression of a return—what influence would she have with him? *I'm your wife* would mean little to him. *As the mother of your son...* a little more, perhaps.

Would she end up begging for his love? Or would she do as she had done with Luigi—simply cut off from that unfulfilled part of her? To cut off from her sexuality had made her cool, self-contained, precise. To cut off from her heart, from her ability to love—that would be a thousand times worse. She could not guess what she would become. Pinched and unforgiving? Hard and cynical?

How would she raise her child if she protected her heart? Children demanded, required, to be loved from a full and open heart. Every child had the right to be raised with love. Could she raise her child in a materially privileged but emotionally arid environment? Did she have the duty, or even the right, to sacrifice her child's happiness in the name of peace between Tamir and Montebello? Or even to give him a father?

This isn't the fourteenth century. Our countries need a peace treaty, not a marriage, Christina's voice said in her memory. And her sister was right. Rashid's dream of peace through marriage was just that—a dream. Their marriage was not a necessary prerequisite to peace. It didn't even guarantee peace. And if it didn't achieve that, their children's loyalties would be torn in two.

And what of Rashid's own loyalties? He said he was not bothered by the feud, but could she be sure of it? A hundred and ten years might be nothing if you were comparing it to 1200 years of family history, but it was still three or four generations in real time. That was plenty long enough for family hatred to take unconscious root. Maybe Rashid hardly knew himself how he would react to being married to a Sebastiani.

If she overcame her instinctive rejection of the marriage now, would he thank her down the road?

A sailing yacht streamed past on graceful, effortless wings, giving her a sudden, sharp memory of salt spray and the smell of teak and rope.

And then, without warning, she was remembering Erimos. How beautiful the sunset had been from the beach when they had lain in the aftermath of lovemaking, salt and sand caked, the water whispering up the sand under their exhausted bodies. She had looked at the world with new eyes then, like one reborn. She had felt a part of every grain of sand, every sparkling drop of water that met the rocks and was hurled up into the rich red-gold rays of the sun for a moment of individual glory.

She had felt a part of the sea.

She should have known then that she loved Rashid Kamal.

Chapter 16

*7 February, 1892. Halstead. What a bustle we are in!
Elizabeth and I have new dress fittings every morning
and afternoon. So many gowns and dresses are necessary to a come-out I have lost count. Tea gowns,
ball gowns, and of course the Court Presentation
dress! The train must be exactly three yards long!*

*My own presentation dress is utterly lovely. Papa
has been so generous, writing that when the Princess
of Montebello meets the Queen of England, she
should be dressed as befits the Princess of Montebello! The dress is a deep-lustred silk satin, the entire
skirt quilted over with pearls, the bodice embroidered
with diamonds! The dressmaker who is in charge of
that is very superior, and speaks to the ordinary
dressmakers in tones that Papa would not use to the
meanest street cleaner!*

*We are receiving instruction on how to approach
Her Majesty when the time comes, how deep the curt-*

sey must be, the right moment to kiss her hand, and most important—how to back out of her presence without tripping over our three-yard trains! How humiliating it would be to trip and fall as, we are warned, some ladies have done! Or to forget to kiss her hand! I am sure the presentation at the Court of San Sebastian cannot be anything like as daunting as this. Here the eyes of the whole world are on one. N3 2n4 yw 3 rdd ht yd, rf hc yd rbgns s5 lcrs 4t ht yd hwn brtr dn 3 smt 2b rpdt....

20 February. Halstead. Our plans have had a setback. Dearest Elizabeth has contracted measles and is very uncomfortable. This means we will not go up to Town next week, as planned, but will remain here until she is fully recovered....

21 February. Halstead. I have just received a dreadful shock. His Royal Highness has arrived in England, apparently on my account! He came to Halstead yesterday and insisted on seeing me. Of course I had to go down to him. What a very fine-looking man he is. I am sure he is very deserving of a woman's love, and 3 swh 2h lcd nfd 1 mwn rwhty f4 mh. S1 rf 2m, 6m rht s3 rlyd vgn. Wh rfntt htt brtr sw tn n3 ht sh hwn 2h lcdl!

Rashid had gone to London without her. Julia knew very well that the more she appeared with him in public, the higher would be the expectation of their marriage.

Out of fear that she might weaken, she had called a journalist, and was nervously waiting for the story to appear.

Meanwhile, she was dividing her time between reading

the legible portions of the last diary, and trying to decipher the code the rest was written in. She had the book on codes and was trying the various methods of cryptanalysis suggested in it. She spent most of a morning counting up all the letters in a large passage and applying the number frequency scale in English to it, but nothing came of that. But then for all she knew the original language could be French or German or Italian, all of which languages Delia had been versed in. And the frequency scale was different for each language. *E* was the letter that appeared most often in English, but not in either Italian or French.

3 vl mh. Wh nc 3 rmyr tnrh hwn 6m rht s3 rlyd vgn?

An oddity of the encrypted passages was that they were almost entirely made up of two-, three-, and four-letter clusters. Delia's plain text writing did not have such a limited vocabulary, which suggested that the clustering was a part of the code itself.

But it was completely random. There was no pattern of two, three and four that would suggest what was behind this clustering. And the mixing in of numbers was also unusual, according to the codes the book described.

She had tried a cipher based on the keyword "Julius" without getting anywhere. Next she had tried "Bliss," the name of Delia's mare. The work was tedious and frustrating and she couldn't really be sure she had eliminated those possibilities entirely, which made hunting through the diaries and letters for another possible keyword seem pointless.

"Maybe you're looking in the wrong direction," Rashid said over the phone. He was in London and had phoned her with a progress report.

"The Worthington estate is now owned by Lord Devere," he had told her. "The house and grounds are open to the public. I've booked a private tour of the house and have asked to look at the Worthington family archives. That's on Monday.''

Meanwhile he had visited the records centre and learned the date of Robert Worthington's death. March 20, 1892.

''The day after Delia's suicide!'' Julia cried. ''Oh, but that doesn't make sense! Why did she kill herself, then?''

''It's not what we expected,'' Rashid agreed. ''But I did double-check the date of her death.''

''And it was definitely March 19?'' asked Julia.

''Yes, the family record is correct there.''

''And Omar was killed on the fifteenth. It doesn't fit. Unless Delia was in love with Omar after all. Suppose— suppose Robert killed Omar so he could have Delia and then Delia realized it was Omar she really loved, or felt guilty, and killed herself? And then Robert killed himself in remorse.''

''Maybe she even helped Robert to do it?''

''You think Delia was a Lady Macbeth?''

''It doesn't seem very likely. I'm going to try to check the archives of *The Times* newspaper, to see what was reported at the time. You'd think the death of the second Duke of Rochester in as many years would have caused some ripples.''

''The newspapers! I never thought of that,'' Julia admitted. ''They'd have reported the death of Prince Omar, too, wouldn't they? And the Princess of Montebello's.''

''I'll check it out.''

Next they discussed what she was learning from the diaries and her struggles with the code. And Rashid said, ''Maybe you're looking in the wrong direction. Try another approach.''

''For instance,'' Julia asked, her voice suddenly sad. She was thinking how much effort Rashid was investing in this, for the sake of putting an end to the family feud. He was the first person in four generations to have stood out against the stupid brainwashing that each family operated, passing hatred and bile down to each succeeding generation. This made him a man of truly independent mind. A rare breed.

She herself had bought in to the feud without question. She had taken it in with her mother's milk, a stupid, self-limiting animosity that served no purpose except to fuel discord and misery in the world.

It suddenly occurred to her that if there had been no family feud between the Kamals and the Sebastianis, there could hardly exist the group who called themselves the Brothers of Darkness. How had they managed to operate? By convincing the Sebastianis that their bombs and kidnappings were the work of the Kamals.

Hatred begetting worse hatred.

What fools they had all been, for the past 110 years. All except Rashid. It was no wonder she had fallen in love with him. He was all the things a man should be—noble, dedicated, caring, and above all, a man who thought for himself. He was intelligent, with a sense of humour, and he was determined to make the world a better place. The mystery was how she had been blind to all that.

Her brainwashing fell away from her abruptly, like an old skin. *I can see clearly now the rain has gone.*

But she still couldn't marry him.

"What is it?" Rashid asked, quick to pick up on her mood.

"Just thinking," she said.

"About what, Julia?"

"Nothing."

She wanted to hide it from him. She did not want an argument about marriage, not now.

He gave vent to a little burst of laughter. "Nothing? I don't think so. What's bothering you, Julia?"

She sighed. "I was just thinking about a century of stupidity. There's nothing to say about it. Except—what a waste."

"Does this mean you've given up thinking of me as a Kamal?" Rashid said, his voice urgent.

"I suppose I have," she said. "All of a sudden it just—happened. It's just so bloody stupid. A hundred years of strife for what? Because a girl was in love with the wrong man. Because she wanted personal happiness, wanted to be loved for herself instead of being treated as a pawn in a larger game. It's not a lot to ask, is it?" she said, not realizing how much of a plea was in her voice. "Why couldn't she just have been treated like a human being instead of a title deed?"

"Does this mean you'll marry me?" Rashid said.

"No," said Julia, sad but firm. "No, it doesn't mean that. It means just the opposite, Rashid. I'm sorry."

After that they never got back to discussing Delia's diary code. But what Rashid had said made her try again. Another approach.

Maybe she had been too complicated. Delia had been eighteen years old and writing a diary, not a spy writing secrets. Delia hadn't had to fear that the entire Foreign Office signals staff would be trying to crack her code—she only wanted to protect her thoughts from casually prying eyes.

And she probably hadn't had access to a nice neat book on codes and ciphers like the one Julia was using.

The most significant point, she suddenly realized, was that Delia had written her code mostly in longhand. Any spy using one of the complicated keyword codes would have had to use printing, because each letter had to be looked up separately. But Delia's code must have been easy to memorize, to come so fluidly off her pen.

There were only six numbers used. Julia had combed through the entire diary, and she was almost certain of that. And only two numbers ever appeared as singletons, 1 and 3. Julia's first instinct had been that the six numbers stood for the vowels—*a, e, i, o, u* and *y*. But she had abandoned that hypothesis because if it were right, every word should have had at least one number. But very few of the letter clusters had numbers in them.

Now she decided to try that hypothesis again. She wrote out a line of code.

Brtr sh ds htt 2w smt psk 4t 6m pp, tb 3 rd tn. 3 vh ltd brtr htt 3 smt 4d 6m tdy.

And rewrote it substituting vowels for the numbers, with *A*=1, *E*=2, *I*=3, *O*=4, *U*=5, and *Y*=6.

Brtr sh ds htt EW smt psk OT YM pp, tb I rd tn. I vh ltd brtr htt I smt OD YM tdy.

At first glance it didn't look promising. There was no two-letter word in English starting with the letter *e* except "eh," and none starting with *y* except "ye," both of which were unlikely in the context of Delia's diary. On the other hand, the two singletons became *I*. And there were two words starting with *o*—"on" and "of," perhaps.

She realized suddenly how tense she was. Hunched over and frowning. That wasn't the best way to let intuition flow. Julia consciously relaxed for a few moments, breathing slowly and deeply. Then she let her eyes wander over the line of code. *Delia,* she thought, *come on, Delia, tell me your secret!*

And then her eyes noticed the obvious. If she reversed all the two-letter words in which she had substituted a letter for a number, they were all English words.

WE, TO, MY, DO and MY.

"Okay!" Julia said aloud. "We may be onto something here."

"My husband is a lateral descendant of the last Duke of Rochester, Your Highness," said Lady Ursula as she led Rashid up a massive oak staircase. "His great-grandmother was Robert Worthington's sister, Elizabeth. She inherited the estate under Robert's will. She married Lord Henry Devere, who was a younger brother, in 1895."

She paused on a landing which overlooked the large square stairwell. Here, as everywhere, the walls were covered with portraits by the famous of the famous of generations of a family.

"That is Robert. His portrait was done immediately upon his coming into the title, fortunately, since he inhabited it barely a year before his accident. There are one or two photographs, but not so good a likeness as this."

Rashid and Lady Ursula paused and looked up at the portrait, hung high on one wall. It showed a handsome, fair-haired young man with blue eyes and a charming smile.

"He was twenty-five when he died. A pity he hadn't married," Lady Ursula murmured.

"Is there any record in the family history that at the time of his death he was intending to marry?"

She turned to him in surprise. "No. I've made quite a study of my husband's family, as of course one had to do in order to make a success of all this." She waved a hand towards a tasselled rope that hung across the doorway to a private wing. Like so many of the great houses of England, Halstead House had to open to the public or see the estates sold to pay death duties.

"People want to know the history of the place and the family and I've written most of the guides and brochures

myself. But I've certainly never heard a suggestion of this
before. Do you have a particular reason for the question?''

"I have seen a marriage licence in the duke's name,"
Rashid said.

Lady Ursula, an elegant, slim woman in her early fifties,
stared at him. There was such a fine mixture of surprise
and disbelief in her face that he laughed.

"You've *seen* it! Where? And who was the woman?''

"We found it secreted in the diary of Princess Delia of
Montebello. It is in the royal archive in San Sebastian. It
allowed the marriage of Delia and Robert.''

Ursula blinked. "Princess Delia of Montebello!'' She
stared at him. "She was going to marry Robert? But—wait
a minute, am I remembering the right person? This
can't—''

She turned away and went to a window embrasure where
a large black binder was lying. "We do these information
packs for our guides, you know, in case visitors ask questions about the portraits.''

She quickly flipped over the plastic-sheeted pages in the
binder, till she found what she was looking for. "Here we
are.'' She read aloud.

*"The young man in the portrait on the centre back
wall is Robert Charles Fitzroy Mountalan Worthington, the ninth and last Duke of Rochester. Robert inherited the title from his father in November 1890.
One day in the spring of 1892, Robert's horse came
home with an empty saddle. The searchers were immediately sent out, but Robert staggered home on his
own. He was seriously wounded. He had fallen from
his horse onto his own gun. He lived long enough to
make a will leaving the estate to his sister, Elizabeth,
great-grandmother of the current owner.''*

Ursula looked up. "No, there's nothing there. I know we do have some information about Princess Delia. Of course, the fact that it was a suicide was hushed up completely. I believe it was given out at the time that she had slipped into the river from the little bridge during a rainstorm...." She frowned in the effort to remember. "But surely the reason for her suicide was that her fiancé had been killed?"

"That is what has been believed up until now. The marriage licence has only recently been discovered."

Lady Ursula lifted her eyebrows with sudden intent interest. "You're saying these deaths are linked?"

Rashid made a movement with his chin.

"How did her fiancé die?"

"He was killed in the road—between here and London. The police never solved the murder and were convinced it was merely one in a spate of highway robberies at the time, in spite of the fact that Prince Omar's body had not been robbed of his jewellery or money."

"Prince Omar! Yes, I see the connection now! Omar was your—"

"My great-great-uncle. Like your husband with Robert, I am in a position I would not have inherited if Omar had lived."

"And of course it's been all over the news that you want to marry Princess Julia. Forgive me if this is too personal, but is it true, or just so much tabloid scandalmongering?"

"It is very true. I intend to marry her."

"And trying to solve this old mystery—has it got something to do with that?"

Rashid smiled. "That's right. I'm determined to put this feud to rest. I think we're close to doing that."

"And you think Robert's death may be relevant? Well, it must be, if, as you say, there was a marriage licence!" She paused, tapping her lower lip with a forefinger. "I wonder—did you know that Lord Henry Devere, my husband's great-grandfather, was Robert's best friend at the time of his death?''

Rashid's eyebrows went up. "We didn't know that."

"Harry died in 1941. There's only one member of the family still living who knew him well. Elizabeth died in the 1919 flu epidemic, and Harry remarried. His daughter from that second marriage is still alive.

"I wonder if she could tell you anything."

Brtr sh ds htt WE smt psk TO MY pp, tb I rd tn. I vh ltd brtr htt I smt DO MY tdy.

If these words were simply reversed letters, Julia decided, maybe all of them were reversed. So she wrote, *rtrb hs sd tth WE tms ksp TO MY pp, bt I dr nt. I hv dtl rtrb tth I tms DO MY ydt.*

Then she looked for clues. *To my pp.* "To my Papa!" she cried. "It has to be! You left out the vowels in the larger words, Delia, and put them in numerically in the smallest words. And all the consonants reversed!"

She wrote the sentence again with blanks between the consonants, and then tried to brainstorm meaning.

r-t-r-b h-s s-d t-th WE t-m-s k-s-p TO MY p-p-, b-t I d-r n-t. I h-v d-t-l r-t-r-b t-th I t-m-s DO MY y-d-t.

"Retrib has sad teeth we teams k-s-p to my papa, but I dare not. I have detail retrib teeth I times do my y-d-t," she guessed at random. Then she sat gnawing her lip.

"Some of the words make sense this way," she told Rashid that night over the phone. She had gone to bed early and was reading when he made his now-regular nightly call. She tossed down her book and picked up the notebook she had left on her bedside table in expectation of his call.

"But there are some combinations that just don't have any possible meaning. "Like *ksp* and *ydt*. There's just no combination of letters like that in any English word. I've tried French and Italian, in case she stuck in foreign words, but I can't find anything there, either.''

Rashid made a little noise. "This is very Arabic."

"What?"

"The Arabic writing system leaves out all the vowels, just as Delia has done."

"Really?" Julia was intrigued.

"And even her trick of putting in a vowel signifier where there is only one consonant in a word, such as *to* and *my*, is replicated in Arabic, to avoid making a word of a single consonant."

Julia frowned thoughtfully. "She was a bit of a linguist, she had four languages, do you suppose…does *ksp* mean anything in Arabic?"

"There is no *p* at all in Arabic."

"So that lets that out!"

"That thought makes you happy."

It was true, she couldn't keep the satisfaction from her tone. She wanted to crack this code, and if it were half in Arabic she would have to wait for Rashid's return.

"Well, you can't do all the detective work. This means I can continue on my own."

"Let's not be hasty. What is the other set of letters that puzzled you?"

Obediently she consulted her notebook. "*Ydt.* It's part of a phrase. It comes after *do my.*"

Rashid erupted with laughter. "And you can't get it, Julia? Come on!"

"What do you mean?"

"I'm disappointed in you. Clearly you and Delia had a great deal in common, if only you would realize it. Maybe you have a mental block. *Do my*—and three letters, *d, t,* and *y.*"

She gasped.

"You've got it, have you?"

"*Duty!* Oh, Rashid, this must be it. She's just jumbled the letters or something. I'll work on that."

"Not tonight, it's late."

"No, I'm already in bed."

"Are you ill?" he asked in quick concern.

"I just felt like an early night. I've been reading. I'll put the light out in a minute." She snuggled down into her pillows, the receiver against her ear.

"Put the light out now, while I am talking to you."

She obeyed in silence. He waited till he heard the click.

"Is it dark now, Julia? And are you lying down?"

"Yes."

"I wish I were there with you, Julia," he whispered. "Lying beside you. I wish I could make love with you tonight. If I were there would you make love with me?"

Chapter 17

She bit her lip against the little spiral of yearning in her stomach.

"I want to see you. Let me see you in my mind's eye. What are you wearing, Julia?" he asked with seductive slowness.

Sudden heat rushed up her body at his tone. She bit her lip.

"Tell me."

"A blue nightgown."

"Ah. Does it match your eyes?"

She swallowed. "It's midnight blue."

"It makes your eyes very dark, then. Like the night sky. Like sapphires. Are your eyes like sapphires tonight, Julia?"

"I have no idea," she said, trying to resist the pull.

"I know they are. There's a moon tonight. Can you see it from your bed?"

She always opened the curtains last thing before getting into bed. "I can see the stars."

"So they are reflected in your eyes. I like the stars best when I see them in your eyes, Julia. What is your nightgown made of?"

"Silk."

"Silk." He drew the word out as if tasting it, as if it were some kind of delicious food. "Is there lace to trim it?"

"A little."

"Over your breasts, Julia? Is there lace lying on the swell of your breasts?"

She couldn't resist. She felt herself sucked in as a little whoosh of feeling rushed over her body. Her tiny intake of air was audible to him.

"Tell me."

"Yes," she murmured.

"Your breasts are pressing against the silk. Imagine me there now, Julia, on the bed beside you. Looking at you in starlight, touching you. Can you see me there?"

"Rashid—"

"No, no protests. I draw your arm aside and there are your breasts behind midnight-blue lace, and two perfect beads, just outlined by silk."

Her skin shivered into awareness.

"Put your hand onto your breast, Julia, and imagine it is my hand there, touching you."

"Oh, God!" she whispered helplessly.

"My thumb strokes the nipple gently, so gently, do you feel it? The silk makes a tiny noise as it moves over your breast, a whisper of protest only, and your perfume comes up from your skin. Can you smell the scent of your perfume, Julia?"

She was beyond speech.

"I breathe it in and it makes me drunk. I am kissing you, Julia, your temple, where your heart beats so delicately, your eyelid, down over your nose, your cheek, your ear, and down the line of your neck. My hand is in your hair, drawing it aside so that my lips can go where they wish. More perfume comes from your hair, Julia, every curl is a flower, as I told you before. And every flower breathes its scent into my nose.

"Can you smell it? I can smell you, Julia. My hand is at my lips, but it is you that I kiss. Can you feel my mouth?"

"Rashid…"

"Tell me you can feel my mouth against your throat, there where your heartbeat is. Do you feel my kiss in that soft hollow, Julia?"

"Oh, God!" she whispered. Rivers of sensation were flooding over and through her body. She was melting.

"And your shoulder, I am kissing there, too," he breathed. "My hands on the soft flesh of your arms. Your muscles are firm, Julia, but your curves are all female. Do you know that? Every curve folds into every other with an intoxication that says *woman*."

Her blood was melted gold guided through her body by his voice. "Do you feel my hands on your shoulders, your arms? Holding you tight because you are mine, Julia. Because I can never let you go. Do you know that? I can't let you go."

She swallowed and licked her lips, forming a protest. But her voice did not come.

"My lips have found your breast now, in the darkness. Are you surprised that I can see you by starlight? Ah, but Julia…I will always be able to find you in darkness. Like the poem. If not by your white forehead, then by the music of your ornaments, and if not by that, then by your perfume. By the scent that is only you.''

"Rashid," she protested.

"My mouth is on your breast," he said impatiently. "You feel it there, hot and demanding. My tongue seeking that perfect bead through the silk, making the silk wet with my hunger to taste you. And my hands stroking your body, your arms and shoulders, your back, your waist, your legs…my mouth closes on your nipple now, I can taste it, Julia, that taste that is only you. You can feel me there, hungry against your breast, needing you, Julia, wanting you…

"And now I draw the sheet off your body, and there are your legs, and the midnight-blue silk already drawn half up your thighs. My hand clasps your ankle…your calf…your knee…your thigh.'' She heard his roughened breathing. "And up to your hip. Drawn as if by a magnet to the sachet of spices. I'm lifting the silk now, Julia, and looking at your naked body, and my heart is hammering so hard you can hear it where you are. That is what the sight of your body does to me.

"My hand is there in the silky hair, in the folds of ambergris and myrrh. Spread your legs for me, Julia. Do you feel my hands on your thighs, parting them, so that I can see what I desire?

"My body is hard with hunger. Do you sense it? And my mouth is there now, Julia, searching for the taste of you. Do you feel my lips against your thigh, on your belly, Julia? Tell me, can you feel me there?''

"Yes," she whispered, her voice cracking.

"When I taste you I get more hungry for you, Julia, not less. Can you feel my searching tongue press against you, over and over? Can you feel how my tongue rasps across your flesh? I love this, Julia, your body is like the sweetest of forbidden fruits. My hands are pushing your thighs apart—wider, Julia, stretch wide for me. And my fingers are there, in your soft, sweet folds, and my tongue. Does your body like it? Tell me.''

"Yes," she moaned helplessly. "Yes."

"Say it. Say, 'I like it, Rashid. I like what you do to me.' "

"Oh, Rashid!"

His voice growled in her ear, reminding her of other times when she had heard him so close. "Tell me, Julia. Say it."

She could not resist. "I like it, Rashid."

" 'I like what you do to me.' "

"I like what you do to me, Rashid."

And on the words, her body exploded in a rainbow of pleasure and sweetness, and he drank in the nectar of her cries.

In the morning she awoke in a lazy good humour, smiling to herself and melting all over again with the memory of Rashid's voice. She had dreamt of him. In her dream he had said he loved her.

At that she snapped herself back into the real world. She reminded herself of what Rashid and she had discovered, and dressed quickly, eager to crack Delia's code at last. She was sure she had it within reach now.

But it was Sunday, and she and Anna and her parents always tried to have Sunday breakfast together. Even more so with Lucas gone. They all needed the confirmation of the family bond, and this morning Anna was away. So Julia went down to the little breakfast room where the king and queen were already sitting.

The Sunday *Messenger* was lying on the table.

It's Still NO!—Julia shouted the large headline. Julia

checked on the threshold and then went and sat in her usual seat.

"Darling, have you been giving interviews again?" asked her mother mildly.

"Just the one," she murmured. "Coffee, please, Amelia."

Princess Julia Sebastiani firmly repudiates any suggestion that she and Prince Rashid of Tamir, who is the father of her unborn child, will ever marry.

"It's not in my plans," the princess has told close friends. "I will not marry simply to give my child a father. I am sure the people of Montebello will understand why I want to marry for love next time—if there is a next time."

The princess's mother, Gwendolyn, is well-known to have refused Marcus Sebastiani five times before finally accepting him, but Julia is adamant that she is not playing any kind of game....

"Any particular reason why you and Rashid are fighting this out in the papers?" her father asked, grumpily chewing his toast and honey.

Julia picked up a peach and bit into it. The juice spurted into her mouth. Out on the lawn the sprinklers were covering the grass with diamonds. Everything seemed to sparkle this morning.

"Ask Rashid that one. He's the one who keeps telling them we will. All I do is deny it when they call Bertrand for comment."

Her mother indicated the paper with one elegant hand. "This doesn't sound as if it went through Bertrand, darling."

"No, you're right. I was mad after that comment Rashid

made at the film festival gala and called Antony myself. He said he'd save it for Sunday."

"I'm sorry you and Rashid aren't getting along. He seems to spend a lot of his time here, considering you're not," Gwendolyn said, and Julia blushed self-consciously. She could never explain to her mother that she had called Antony because she was afraid of giving in. "What does he think about this?"

"I doubt if he's seen it. He's in England at the moment."

"And what's he doing there?" her father wanted to know.

"It's part of our investigation of Delia's story, though I think he has other business there, too. I've almost cracked her diary code, by the way. I'm hoping I'll have it in the bag today."

Her mother sat up. "Really! Darling, how on earth did you manage that?"

Her parents had merely shaken their heads over the complex codes in the book she had showed them.

"It's actually a dead simple code, that's how. All she did was drop out the vowels and reverse or jumble the letters. There may be some kind of pattern in the jumbling, but if not, I'm hoping it won't be too time-consuming just to try every arrangement of the letters till something comes up."

"And when you've done that, Julia," said the king, "will you be able to convince King Ahmed to withdraw his claim to Delia's Land?"

"We hope so."

"This 'we' is you and Rashid?"

"Yes."

"But you say you're not going to marry him?"

"No. Not—well, no."

"I have to say, Julia—" he began, but stopped abruptly

and cleared his throat. "All right, all right, I won't say anything!" he muttered. Julia turned and was just too late to intercept her mother's look.

"I think, my love, that we can leave Rashid and Julia to sort out their own affairs," Gwendolyn remarked.

Brtr sh ds htt WE smt psk TO MY pp, tb I rd tn. I vh ltd brtr htt I smt DO MY tdy.

If Rashid was right, and *tdy* was *duty,* then the first two consonants had been reversed. Julia tried that first.

rbtr hs sd tht WE mst spk TO MY PAPA, bt I dr nt. I hv tld rbtr tht I mst DO MY DUTY.

It was as easy as a crossword puzzle.

r-b-t-r HAS SAID THAT WE MUST SPEAK TO MY PAPA, BUT I DARE NOT. I HAVE TOLD r-b-t-r THAT I MUST DO MY DUTY.

Julia gave a squeak of delight. *r-b-t-r* must be *Robert.* If the pattern held good, and the first two consonants had been reversed, then so had the last two. But since there were two *r*'s in the word, it wasn't certain. She opened the diary at random and attacked another sentence to test her hypothesis.

Hts nvgn, tsdngn t1 ht hssp lr, brtr kt 6m nhd dn ksd 2m 4t rmyr mh. 3 hthgt 6m rht lwd rbts.

She copied it, filling in the words with numbers replacing vowels and reversing each pair of consonants.

Ths vnng, stndng at th shps rl, Robert tk my hnd nd skd me to mrry hm. I thght my hrt wld brst.

This evening, standing at the ship's rail, Robert took my hand and asked me to marry him. I thought my heart would burst.

"Eureka!" cried Julia.

I told him that it was hopeless. I explained about Prince Omar. He was wild with regret and anger. He blamed himself very deeply, for not declaring himself before I left England. He says that he thought me too young. He believed that as a gentleman he must wait until I was officially out before declaring himself. It is for my sake that he came to Montebello to escort his sister back to England. He said he had not intended even now to speak to me, but we were walking the deck in moonlight and his love overcame him. I showed him the ring Prince Omar gave me and he all but threw it into the sea. I have never seen his face so white. His eyes blazed as he looked at me, and he swore that I was destined to be his wife and no one else's.

I know I should have refused to listen. I should not have confessed how deeply, and how long, I have loved him. But my heart would not allow me to dissemble when he pressed me. For a moment, how close the stars seemed!

He has given me his own ring. It is a circlet of diamonds, a little too big for my finger, but I cannot be seen to wear it. I have put it on my gold chain. It will lie against my heart forever.

Julia sat back, shaking her head. It was painful to witness the birth of tragedy, even when it had come to fruition 110 years ago. Her heart beat hard with a sense of urgency. She wanted to cry to the young lovers, *Lower a lifeboat and escape somewhere they'll never find you!*

To decode the whole diary would be work. For the moment she contented herself with stopping here and there at random to read a passage. Now she had the knack of it, it was possible to read the diary with fair fluency.

February 4. I have been very foolish. I wanted to be able to wear Robert's ring on my finger—only in private—and so I enquired of Lady Worthington the name of a London jeweller. I wanted to have it done without telling Robert. I was writing the instructions to the jewellers, Barratt and Runyon, to cut it to size, when a wild idea occurred to me. I didn't stop to consider, but wrote to them, "and in addition, please take the ruby from the second enclosed ring and set it in the centre of the diamonds".

I sent the package off with my servant without reflecting. It was wrong of me, very wrong. I know that I should not have done it. It is something that can never be explained to Prince Omar. But it is done, and I will not send again to cancel my order. My father and Prince Omar command my duty, but they cannot command my heart.

February 16. Mssrs. Barratt and Runyon have returned the ring. I showed it to Robert, saying, this ruby is my heart, and the diamonds are yours. You have captured my heart as surely as this, and when I take the vows duty forces me to make, I will wear this ring. The prince will have my person, but you have my heart forever.

He was deeply moved and urged me again to fly with him. He says my duty is to him, who loves me. Oh, how I wish I knew the truth of what I should do.

March 3. I have written Julius, begging him, if he knows a way, to help me escape from this marriage.

As Delia's doom crept closer, Julia found herself deeply affected. She had been there herself. She had felt what Delia felt, except that for her there had been no handsome duke to offer another way. She had merely wanted out, and not found the courage to get out.

And for the first time since it had all happened, she had the strength to go and confront her father. First she told him Delia's story, as she had so far deciphered it.

Then she read him some excerpts verbatim from the diary. Times when Delia recorded her struggles with her conscience, her sense of duty to her father. Her grief at facing a marriage that held no hope of happiness for her.

Her father sat in silence, listening. His face was grave, almost as if he knew what was coming.

"Papa," she said gently, "this is how I felt, on the eve of my wedding seven years ago. Do you think it is right that a girl should feel like this before committing herself to a man for life?"

There was a long, pregnant silence.

"No, Julia," he said. "No, I don't think it right."

"Papa, why did you so desperately want me to marry Luigi? What was in it for you? I have a right to ask, don't you think?"

Her father bowed his head. "You have a right to ask. I only wish I could give you a clear-cut answer. I don't think I can. If you're hoping to hear me say that Mario di Vitale

Ferrelli had a hold over me or something like that, it's not the case.

"I thought I was acting in your best interests. You are a beautiful and passionate young woman, Julia. And you are a princess. You were just coming into the public eye at nineteen, and I knew it would not be long before you..." He faded off.

"I was afraid that you would get hurt. In the way that Christina afterwards was, by a young man with fewer scruples than you gave him credit for. I thought how terrible it would be for you if a young man revealed the details of your relationship in the press. I wanted to protect you from that."

She looked at him sadly. "I don't say you're wrong. Maybe some sort of scandal was inevitable. But at least if you'd let me choose my own road to hell I might have had some happiness first. As it was, Papa, I had five unbearable years and then the scandal anyway. Everything Luigi said about me in that awful interview was a lie. I think I'd have preferred it the other way."

"It was foolish of me. Worse than foolish. Your mother told me it could not be done, that you had to be allowed to make your own mistakes. But to my eternal shame I didn't listen."

She was silent, taking it in. "Why Luigi?" she asked after a minute.

"I chose Luigi because he was of good family and I knew that you already liked each other. And he was handsome, too. That was the basis for my choice. You seemed to think that there were other reasons and I allowed you to think so because...well, I hardly remember the why of it now."

"But later, Papa, when I begged you to let me be free? Before we were actually married. When I explained that we could never have a good marriage. What were your reasons then?"

"How many times since that interview I have asked myself what possessed me, Julia. I told myself you were merely panicking, like any young bride at the approach of marriage. I wanted to protect Christina, it's true, but I also thought of you. I thought—a foolish conceit in the modern world, I know—I thought in marriage lay safety."

"But Papa, I was pleading with you. How could you have thought that a marriage I didn't want could be safe for me, for you, for anyone?"

He bowed his head. "I have no answer, Julia. It was a moment of weakness I have regretted over and over. It was a fixed idea. I know now that you tried to shake me from it, but that is the nature of fixity, that one can't be shaken. I hope that your marriage was not always so terrible as the final months were."

She licked her lips, debating with herself. Then she said, "Would it surprise you to know that—that before that night with Rashid Kamal I was a virgin?"

Marcus closed his eyes and went very still. "I did wonder if…but I hoped that the marriage had merely degenerated. That Luigi was capable of love with both men and women."

"It was never a marriage," she said, and she had the satisfaction, if that was what it was, of seeing her father tremble. "We shared nothing except the front we put up in public."

There was a long moment of silence between father and daughter. Then King Marcus heaved a sigh and looked up.

"Julia, if there is one thing I am sorry for more than any other, it is this—that I used your love of me against you. That was my great sin. That I played upon your love and your sense of duty. I used the fact that you wanted to do what was right. That was very gravely wrong, and I am deeply sorry."

Tears sprang to her eyes. It was what she needed to hear from him. "Thank you, Papa."

"In such cases, I see now, though I wouldn't have then, children should resist such emotional blackmail, for that is what it is."

Julia smiled and sniffed.

"Maybe I should have run away, like Delia."

"Did Delia run away?"

"I'm not sure yet, but I think maybe she did. When we've translated all of it, we'll know better. Or maybe not. She didn't write her diary for the last few days. Rashid may find out something."

"That leads me to what I want to say next. If your choice has lighted upon Rashid Kamal, Julia, if you love him, you must not think of me, or the political situation. You must do what is right for you and for your child."

"I'm not—I can't marry him, Papa."

"No? And yet it seems to me—what I hear in your voice when you speak to and of him, Julia, sounds very close to love."

"He doesn't love me. Neither did Luigi. I won't go through that again for any money, Papa. You don't know how—how destructive it is. It makes you not yourself."

He blinked at her. "Rashid doesn't love you? But why is he taking such trouble to uproot the source of the feud, except that he is determined to marry you?"

"He wants—he wants a marriage to solve the feud and bring peace. And I guess he wants his son. I'm just a necessary part of a much larger package."

She was crying in earnest now. Her father stood up and drew her into his arms, letting her weep against his shoulder.

* * *

"Who is it, Ursula?"

"I've brought a young man to see you, Alice. His name is Rashid Kamal. He is the Crown Prince of Tamir. Rashid, this is Lady Alice Devere."

"Rashid Kamal." The old woman blindly put out her hand and grasped his, when he offered it, in a firm handshake. "I wondered if you would come before I died."

Chapter 18

"The hair stood up on the back of my neck," Rashid told Julia the next night. He had flown directly back to San Sebastian and they were walking together on the clifftops overlooking the sea.

Julia had goosebumps just hearing him report it. "Did she tell you something interesting?"

"Very interesting. But tell me what you have learned from the diaries first. What I learned is what comes after the diary stopped, and I want to know how it fits in."

Julia took a breath. "Well—I've skimmed or read most of the last two diaries now, and a lot of it we have more or less guessed."

"Tell me the story from the beginning."

"From what they both tell each other afterwards, Delia and Robert fell in love the first time they met, which was at Delia's first visit to Halstead with Elizabeth. Delia, of course, was obliged to keep her love secret, and didn't know either how to hide it or how to let him know, as a more experienced woman would have done. Robert told her he did believe she loved him, but felt it wrong to declare himself when she wasn't even officially out yet. But once she had gone back home, he began to fear that he'd been a fool. He was afraid circumstances would prevent her promised return to London.

"So he went travelling and fetched up near Montebello as if more or less by chance, and telegraphed Elizabeth that he would come there and escort her back to London. And in late January, that's what he did.

"They sailed to France and then by train and then another ferry and another train went to London. On board the *Queen of Montebello* from Montebello to Marseilles, Delia and Robert were left alone together because Elizabeth and the maid were seasick, and Robert was overcome by his feelings and proposed.

"Delia told him that she was already engaged to Prince Omar, and showed him the ring. But she also confessed her own love. Robert was barely stopped from flinging that heirloom pigeon's blood ruby into the Mediterranean. He insisted that they must find a way to put an end to the engagement so that Delia could marry him.

"He hadn't come equipped with a ring, because he had planned to wait until after Delia's court presentation to propose. But he took off his own ring and insisted she accept it. Delia promised to wear it on a necklace, under her clothes, which she did.

"They got back to Halstead House and preparations went into full swing for the girls' debut. Then in late February everything was delayed because Elizabeth went down with the measles. In the meantime, Delia was horrified when Omar turned up in England. He had chased after her from Montebello, convinced that she had been carried off against her will. He believed she loved him but that her father, having agreed to the marriage and dowry, was now trying to back out of the arrangement, in order to keep the lucrative new copper field in the family.

"Delia of course didn't know how to handle this interview. She was extremely distressed by it, the more so because Omar demanded to know why she wasn't wearing his ring. He forced her to go and put it on, and then was absolutely astonished when he saw what she had done with it. And of course she had no explanation for what she had done."

Rashid frowned. "What had she done?"

"Oh, I forgot to tell you! The mystery of the ring is solved!" Julia cried, and explained.

"Poor Omar," Rashid commented.

"Around this time, I imagine, Delia started writing openly to Julius about Robert. I think the reason we can't find those letters is because Julius wisely burned them. Eventually Delia begged Julius to go and see Omar and get her out of the engagement.

"And as we already knew, he and Ugo did go, and Omar flung them downstairs. Delia was in despair, and told Robert. Robert insisted that they should run away and get married, but Delia refused again."

"I feel for Robert."

"The last entry in the diary, frustratingly, is in plain text on the fourteenth of March, and merely says that Elizabeth, who is still ill, has asked her to visit a poor tenant family about whom she was particularly concerned because the young mother was about to give birth again. Delia remarks that she is to go the next day, March 15, and take some clean linens for the lying-in and some soup."

She finished speaking, and they stood for a moment in the starry night, watching the lights of the boats at sea, and the moon melt its white gold on the black deep.

"She stood here," Julia murmured. "On the night after she first met Prince Omar, Delia stood here and looked out and tried to calm her heart, and subdue it to her duty. And begged to be released from such duty if it were possible."

"Did she?" Rashid asked softly. His voice was a murmur on the wind.

"Yes. She writes about it. She stood just here and prayed. And there was a ship going by, all lighted up." She made a small sound of resigned laughter. "There must be something about this place. I did exactly the same just before my marriage to Luigi."

"You prayed?"

She nodded.

Rashid shook his head. "In those few weeks of the preparation of your marriage, I fought a constant deep urge to come and speak to your father. I believed that if your engagement were a love match, you and Luigi would have been married long before. An engagement lasting over two years meant to my mind an engagement without much love involved. I had long been expecting to see it break up. And I told myself, if she is going to marry a man she doesn't love, it might as well be me."

She laughed in astonishment. "Really? But you didn't do it."

"I lacked the courage of my own inner conviction. I was afraid of looking a fool, or worse. Of being accused of playing the role of saboteur...."

"Yes, it wouldn't have been easy. I wonder what Papa would have done if you'd come."

"And you, Julia, what would you have done?" he murmured.

Another little laughing breath. "I don't know. Fallen on your neck, probably!" She thought of how she had melted when he touched her for the first time in the château. If that chemistry had been there seven years ago, before she had had so much practice in self-control…

She sensed dangerous territory ahead, and in another voice, said, "Your turn now. Tell me what Lady Alice told you."

"You have been expecting me?" Rashid had asked the old woman in surprise.

"For a long time I expected your father, or one of his brothers. But as time went on that became less and less likely," said Lady Alice. She was delicate, even frail. She sat on a divan, very upright, with her back to a large window. Her blue eyes gazed unseeingly into his face. "Eventually I knew it would be you or no one."

"What do you have to tell me?"

"You'd better sit down, young man. You may safely leave us, Ursula."

When she had gone, Lady Alice turned to the prince. "How much do you already know?" she asked.

"Not very much. That Robert Worthington and Delia Sebastiani were in love."

"Yes, they were. Harry Devere was Robert Worthington's best friend, and he knew the secret.

"My father made a second marriage rather late. My mother was a young woman who had seen all her young suitors killed in the war, and I suppose she was thrilled when Lord Harry Devere asked her, though he was then in his fifties. He had been quite a dashing young man, and that reputation stuck. So no doubt she felt she had got a pretty good deal. I was her only child, and she died when I was still a child."

Rashid murmured something, accepting that she would tell her story in her own way.

"My fiancé was killed early in the second war," she

said. "I was living here with my father, before the place was commandeered by the army. The others were all engaged in the war effort and came home only occasionally. Harry was ill and there was no one to nurse him—the servants had mostly gone to war, too. So here we were. I looked after him and together we listened to the progress of the war on the wireless.

"His doctor told him there wouldn't be any recovery. The war wasn't a time when you could lie about a thing like that. Harry had to know.

"My father began to talk about the past. And this one incident from his youth bothered him very much. He said he had to set the record straight before he died. So he told me. It was the story of how Prince Omar of Tamir was killed."

Rashid caught his breath.

"Yes." The old woman nodded. "I wrote it all down and he signed it. You can have that paper, since I can't think of anyone who has more right to it. But if you like I'll tell you the story as he told it to me."

"Please do," said Rashid.

Behind her head clouds were gathering in the summer sky, and a sprinkle of rain pattered the window. The room was suddenly darker.

"It's clouding over, is it?" said Lady Alice. "I can still see light and shade."

"Yes, it's clouding over," he said.

"Harry Devere and Robert Worthington had been best friends from the time they were both at Eton together. It was not a good time to be at any English public school, so much abuse, but Harry said that the two of them managed to get through it pretty well. Robert was a year or two older and he was able to shield Harry from a lot of what went on. Harry was forever grateful to him for that. He said that after that he'd have done anything Robert Worthington asked of him.

"So when Robert came to him to say he needed Harry's help, Harry was all go. Robert had got a special licence in Town, and he was going to abduct Delia Sebastiani and marry her. She was engaged to Prince Omar, which only the family knew, as it wasn't yet official. But Harry said it was obvious to him that she was head over ears in love with the duke. So he had no qualms about helping Robert.

"Well, they waited for an opportunity, and it came one day when Robert learned Delia was to visit a poor family on a distant part of the estate, on Elizabeth's behalf. She was to go in a closed carriage, and when she got in she hardly noticed the coachman—it was Harry, all dressed up in the right gear and disguising his voice, and thinking this a great lark, as he said.

"Delia made her visit, and climbed back into the carriage, and Harry set off. They went down the road a bit and there was Robert walking his horse. Harry, in his guise as coachman, pulled up. Robert explained to Delia that his horse had gone lame while he was out shooting rabbits, and of course it ended with him tying the horse to the back of the carriage and getting in with her.

"Now Harry turned the carriage towards London. He doesn't know when Delia realized that they weren't heading home, but he knew Robert had the marriage licence in his pocket and he didn't think Delia would protest too bitterly when she was told she was his prisoner and going to marry him. His task was to drive them to St. George's, Hanover Square without stopping.

"They were close to London, Harry said, when disaster struck. A carriage travelling in the opposite direction pulled in to let them pass. Harry had no idea the driver was Prince Omar. But Omar would have seen the Worthington coat of arms on the panel of the carriage and doubtless caught sight of Delia through the window as it passed. He turned around and followed them, eventually passing the carriage again. Then he turned around on the road ahead of them and forced Harry to stop his team.

"Omar was outraged to see that Delia was alone with Robert in the coach. He ordered her to get out and into his own carriage, but Robert refused to allow it and commanded her to stay.

"Now, there had been a spate of highway robberies in and around London over the previous few months, and everyone had taken to carrying arms in their carriages. Omar pulled out a pistol and, pointing it at Robert's head, ordered Delia to descend. Harry quickly picked up the shotgun the coachman carried in his seat, and before Omar knew what was what, he was covered, too.

"Robert then pulled out his own pistol.

"So there they were, in a standoff—Robert and Harry levelling at Omar, Omar at Robert. Robert and Omar started to argue, while Delia, Harry said, never spoke a word. They were on a small road, and Harry remembered praying for some farmer on a cart to come along and defuse the situation before it exploded.

"But a fox leaping out of the hedgerow under the nose of Omar's horses set it off. Omar's horses started, and Omar's gun fired. Robert and Harry fired automatically. Omar was hit in the head and chest and fell back dead in his carriage. All the horses bolted, Harry's team in one direction, Omar's in the other.

"Harry struggled to bring the team under control, and finally brought them to a standstill. He called down to ask if his passengers were all right, but the only answer was Delia calling for help. He jumped down and opened the door, and there was Robert lying unconscious and Delia, who had ripped up her petticoat, trying to staunch the blood from a chest wound.

"He said any other woman would have been in hysterics, but not Delia. She told him calmly, 'He's been hit, Harry. Can you turn back to Halstead?'"

Lady Alice fell silent for a moment. Rain drove against the window in a sudden gust. Out the window behind her head Rashid could see one wing of the ancient house. The view had probably not changed since Delia's day.

"Harry said that Robert's colour was good, and so his first thought was to avoid the awkward questions that going to a strange doctor would have occasioned. He helped Delia to bandage Robert, then turned the carriage around and headed back here to Halstead House.

"It was a journey of about an hour. And en route Harry realized that there was going to be the devil of a scandal if it emerged that Prince Omar had been killed in a shootout with the Duke of Rochester. So as he drove, he told me, he conceived of a plan. Once they got close to Halstead property, he stopped the carriage again and told Delia his plan. Then he untied Robert's horse, which was still running behind the carriage, and slapped it on the rump to send it galloping off.

"When they arrived here, Delia, covering her bloody dress with her cloak, jumped down from the carriage and went inside as if nothing had occurred. Harry said he never in his life saw courage like Delia's.

"He drove around to the stables, and the butler was already waiting there, under Delia's instructions. It was almost dark. Together the two men smuggled Robert into the house without anyone else realizing what was going on. They put him to bed, and when he was undressed Harry realized Robert's condition was far more serious than he'd believed. The family doctor, fortunately, was due to make a visit to Elizabeth, who was ill at the time, apparently.''

"She had measles," Rashid said.

"Ah, was that it. Fortunate, but it wasn't enough. The doctor saw Robert, again with no servant in the house being the wiser. His loyalty to the family was unquestioned. Elizabeth and her mother, of course, were told, but none of the servants were enlisted to help.

"It wasn't long before Robert's horse showed up at the stable and the alarm went up. The searchers were sent out in the usual way. After an hour or two they called the searchers in. They pretended that Robert had staggered home, wounded but still on his feet. They called the doctor again, all that. The story they gave out was that Robert's horse had bolted and he had fallen onto his own gun, and it had fired, wounding him.

"When the news spread the next day that Prince Omar had been found shot dead in a ditch near London with his horses and carriage nearby, no one even thought of connecting the two incidents. And of course there was absolutely no evidence. Omar's horses had taken him away from the actual scene.

"They nursed Robert for several days. He did regain consciousness. They were overjoyed, thinking he would recover after all, but Robert knew he would not recover, and he insisted on making out his will, leaving the estate to Elizabeth.

"He spoke to his mother, and to his sister, and then to Harry. My father didn't tell me what Robert said to him in that interview. But I've wondered since if he perhaps gave his blessing to the marriage of Harry and Elizabeth. After all, as a younger son, Harry's prospects weren't good. And Elizabeth was a great heiress.

"Lastly he spoke to Delia. A few hours later he slipped

into unconsciousness again. The doctor said that he had only hours to live.

"Princess Delia must have slipped out of the house late that night. Her body was found the next morning, in the river that runs through the estate. There was a storm in the night, and the bridge was damaged. It was given out that she had lost her footing on the bridge when she was out taking an early-morning walk.

"Robert lasted all that day and died the next, without regaining consciousness again. And the secret has been kept to this day."

Julia stood looking out into the darkness as Rashid's voice faded. The night was warm all around them.

"Poor Delia," she said. "Imagine how she felt, in that carriage, with Robert telling her he was taking matters into his own hands. She must have been so happy. And then, a few minutes later…"

They were silent, watching a ship pass on the water.

"I visited her grave," Rashid said at last. "She's buried not far from Robert, in the little churchyard in the village."

"Is she?" Julia murmured. "I'm glad they were together at last."

"So we have solved the mystery together, Julia. We have put an end to our family's hundred-year war."

"Have you told your father?"

"Yes, by telephone, from England. He is waiting for my return with the documentation. We expect to hold a press conference next week. My father will formally withdraw the accusation over Omar's death and any claim to blood money or to Delia's Land. He hopes to invite your father to join him at the press conference."

"So it's over," she said quickly, not wanting to face what was coming next.

"And what about us, Julia? Shall we be together at last, you and I?"

Her heart began to pound with heavy thuds of anxiety. If only he could see...but his next words proved that Rashid had not moved from his original position.

"Shall we join them at the press conference, to announce the sealing of the peace with our coming marriage? This is my fourth proposal, Julia. My father has told me of your latest announcement in the press, rejecting me. I hope it will be the last.

"I know you do not love me, Julia, but I think we could make a good marriage. Many people have started out with less than what we share and made a marriage which worked."

"What do we have?" she asked quietly.

"We enjoy each other's company, don't we? We laugh together and we work together. And we have made a child together." His voice sounded strained, but it was too dark to see his face. "We also have two nations that want to live in peace. My father hopes that our son can be made the heir to the throne of both our countries, so that in fifty years or so Tamir and Montebello will become one nation.

"There is every reason for us to marry, Julia. So I ask you again, for the fourth time, will you marry me?"

She took a deep breath and wrestled with temptation. He still did not guess the truth. Couldn't she marry him pretending it was for all the reasons he had just outlined, and hope that, over time, he would come to love her?

She loved him. She loved him with a depth she hadn't believed existed. Her soul yearned to his. And he was the most honourable man she had ever met. Even if he never actually fell in love with her, she was sure she could trust him to treat her well....

Her head was shaking a negative even as the thoughts

passed through her mind. "I'm sorry, Rashid. I can't believe a marriage without love would work. Maybe if I hadn't tried it once already, I'd have more hope. But I know that it just…eats away at the soul."

He tried to speak, but his voice caught. He coughed. "Are you so sure you would never learn to love me? In spite of all that we share, you think it would be impossible?"

The ache in her heart was too great to bear, suddenly, and Julia cracked. A half laugh escaped her, and it all came pouring out. "Rashid, can't you see? Can't you understand? I already love you! It's because I love you that I can't agree to a political marriage, not because I don't! Can't you see how rejection—"

She broke off because he had grasped her arms, pulling her towards him with a little jerk.

"What?" he said, his voice a deep, almost inarticulate growl. "What did you say? You love me?"

"Yes!" she cried, astonished by what a relief it was to say it. "Yes, of course I love you! If only I'd realized it, I fell in love with you that night in the château, when you lifted me up and I didn't know who you were. Your arms were so…so sure, and I felt as if I'd come home."

"And this is the reason you have refused to marry me? Because *you love me?* Am I crazy, or are you?"

The moon was rising over the sea now, and she could see starlight reflected in his eyes, his jaw tense with feeling.

"You don't understand," she said, wishing now she hadn't spoken, because she was so close to tears and it would be impossible to put her case. "You don't love me, so you don't know—"

"Don't love you? Don't *love you?* What do you think has been motivating me, you little fool? Of course I love you! You know that I have wanted to marry you for over ten years! Why do you speak such nonsense to me?''

Julia's knees buckled. She would have fallen if his grip had not been so merciless on her arms. ''You—what?'' she whispered.

''Not love you? I have been mad for love of you! Do you think I put our whole enterprise at risk that night at the château—an enterprise involving many nations and months of planning—do you think I put that at risk for…for…'' Words failed him. ''What do you imagine?''

''I don't know,'' she managed to whisper.

''You don't know! I have just told you how tortured I was in the weeks before your marriage, how I imagined going to your father, putting a stop to it—what does a man have to say to a woman?''

''But why didn't you tell me?''

''Tell you? I have told you nothing but the fact that I love you! Why do you think I have moved heaven and earth to uncover the mystery of Omar's death? From the first moment that I realized all was not as history had reported, when I understood that perhaps I could put an end to this nonsense by uncovering the truth so that you could stop hating the Kamal and start to see the Rashid in me—I have devoted myself to the task! What kind of statement did you need?''

''But…you kept saying it was for political reasons.''

''I put forth the reasons I thought might sway you, even against your instinctive revulsion for a Kamal. I never said they were my own! Every word I have spoken to you, every time I reached for you, kissed you—from the beginning this has been love! How could you not know it?

''You—*Allah,* let me hear it again! You love me? Say it! Tell me it was the truth, Julia!''

So much emotion swept her that she could hardly stand. Joy and fear and delight...

"I love you, Rashid," she said.

His arms enclosed her and his mouth found hers, and the night sky exploded with stars.

Chapter 19

In the early hours of the morning, they lay in her bed in the palace in San Sebastian, a Kamal and a Sebastiani, entangled in each other, body and spirit. Outside the stars glittered in the velvet sky. Across the room a lamp gave the room a soft glow.

"Why didn't you tell me you loved me long ago?" Julia asked again, her finger toying with his ear, tracing the beloved line of his cheek and jawbone, pressing his chin.

"I did not know it myself, at first," Rashid said, catching her finger between his lips and rubbing his tongue over the tip. "Afterwards, I thought I did tell you. How many times does a man have to propose before he is understood to have love on his mind?"

"But you said you only wanted marriage for the sake of peace."

He rolled onto his back, drawing her onto his chest. "A man can be self-deluded, can't he?" She lay with her back arched, looking down into those dark, dangerous eyes.

"And when did you know that it was love?" she wanted to know.

His hand stroked lovingly all along the smoothly muscled spine down to her rump, and back again. "I think I almost realized it on Erimos. We had enjoyed such love-making, such closeness, and yet still, next morning, you said you would never marry me. A kind of fire burned up in my head, something I had never felt before. And when that finally cooled, I was able to see the truth."

"Which was that you love me."

"That I had loved you for years. I saw you once when you were about sixteen, at some sort of charity function, I have forgotten which. You made a short speech, presenting someone with an award. You were completely beautiful. A simple dress, your hair down, and your face with such promise of beauty and tenderness. The beauty of a woman with a mind, and a soul, and a conscience.

"Like that photograph of Delia, you were all potential. And it was then that I told myself, for the first time, that marriage with you would bring peace to our countries. I didn't realize what that said about my feelings. I suppose I didn't want to know that I loved you, because I was so likely to be rejected. So I thought instead—she will be a fine queen, and we will make a peace."

She could vaguely remember that night. "But you didn't do anything about it?"

"There was nothing to do at that time. You were at school in Switzerland. Like Robert Worthington, I thought it better to wait. But I waited too long. You came home after your final year, and in a very short time your engagement was announced."

As if the thought displeased him still, he lifted his head to kiss her throat and trailed his possessive mouth down her breastbone. Her skin was still all alive with his love-making, and she shivered.

"I said to myself, well, I have missed the boat. Then for two years nothing happened, and finally I imagined that the engagement would not last. I was just thinking the time was coming for it to be broken off, when the date of your wedding was announced."

She was surprised into a half-gasping laugh. "I did try to break it off, so you were right. But events intervened."

"And then those nights when I half believed I should present myself to your father...they were tormented nights. I wanted to do it, but logic and reason told me not to be such a fool.

"And so you were married. And after five years you were divorced. Now, I said to myself—this time I will have her."

"And all this time you didn't think you loved me?"

Rashid smiled. "I had seen you so rarely. You were half a dream to me. I thought the dream was one of peace, not one of personal happiness."

"And then Mariel's wedding in the château," she said.

His eyes darkened with the memory. "And even then I wondered what had come over me, why I had been so over-whelmed.... You fell asleep, and I had to leave. I had to leave you without a word. I knew no message was possible—anything like that might jeopardize our mission. I stood looking down at you lying there in the lamplight....

"A virgin. You had been a virgin. I don't know how I kept the knowledge from myself then, that what swept me was love. I remember feeling a bottomless gratitude that in spite of everything you were mine, all mine."

His voice grated on feeling, and her heart leapt.

"And then to hear that you were pregnant, when I was far away and could not allow myself to call you or send you any kind of message. Julia, I thought it would tear my heart out. I imagined you alone, facing your father with the facts, perhaps thinking I had deliberately abandoned you. And my own father making those outrageous demands, firing up the feud that I wanted ended.

"I was afraid of what you would do. I worried that if my father kept it up you might terminate the pregnancy."

She gasped. "Oh, I could never have done that!"

Rashid shook his head. "I lived with the fear that, one way or another, I would never see my son. Then they said that you were going on a tour of the States. I thought, how can they ask this of her? She is pregnant, she will be a target for the *Ikhwan*—the Brothers of Darkness. Because I *knew*, as you did not, that it was not the Kamals who were behind the kidnap attempts. I was ferociously angry with whoever had set it up, imagining what horrors would happen to you if the kidnappers struck again, and succeeded."

She smiled. "You know what? It—"

"It was not you. I know."

Julia opened her mouth in surprise. "How did you know that?"

Rashid laughed aloud. "How did I know? Am I blind? I had held you in my arms! She looked like you, but she was not you. How can I explain it? You carry your head like a flower on a stem, Julia, every movement makes it tremble. Every movement catches my heart. The woman I saw on the news was beautiful, but she did not touch my heart. Except as she reminded me of you.

"But even then I did not know myself. I came home, determined to put everything right, and with another fine excuse for marrying you. You were pregnant. You needed me. When the truth was, I needed you."

She couldn't help the smile that spread across her face.

Rashid watched her mouth tremble and then curl up at the corners, and was lost. He drew her down to his hungry kiss, and for a long moment they did not speak.

"But you did not need me," he continued. "As you were quick to tell me. You shouted at me to get my white horse out of your life. I was so furious, Julia! My grand gesture hurled back in my face with such contempt! You could not expect me then to realize that what I felt was love. *A loveless marriage,* you said. *Because you do not love me, and I do not love you.*"

"Did I say that?" she asked with a gamine grin. "What an idiot I can be."

"My sister tried to tell me that my feelings were involved, but I would not believe it. Then slowly it crept up on me, like the sea. One night my mother said, *Let her find someone who loves her. And maybe you should find a woman you can love the way Omar loved Delia.* Something like that. And then I knew, and it was no surprise. It was as if I had always known it. Like one of those optical illusions. You are staring at it and staring at it, and when the image finally forms…it is a strange realization. You see that it was there all along.

"My heart said that I had already found the woman I loved. I could not let her find another man who loved her, because that would kill me. I had to win her for myself."

She lowered her head towards the full, strong mouth, and his hand came up, firm, protective, possessive, to cup her head and hold her there for his kiss. Smiling with desire, she resisted another moment.

"And that's when you decided to end the feud once and for all?"

"I wanted to cut all the ground from under your feet. I knew I had to make my father see reason, make him withdraw from this ridiculous claim for ancient blood money.

And there was only one chance for me. That strange ring gave me hope that there was something in Omar and Delia's story worth uncovering.''

"And how right you were! Poor Delia! But you know, I have a sneaking suspicion that if she hadn't already met and fallen in love with Robert, she could have been very attracted to Omar. Even in her worst moments with him, she can't help admitting what an attractive man he is.''

"I am glad you think so," Rashid said, drawing her irresistibly down to within reach of his mouth.

"Now, my Beloved," he murmured, when she lifted her head again. "I ask you one more time. The fifth time. Will you marry me?''

She wanted to joke, but the look in his eyes knocked all the breath out of her body. She licked her lips.

"Tell me your answer," he commanded.

And she smiled, with all the love of her heart shining in her eyes, and told him what he wanted to hear.

Julia Says Yes At Last!
Princess Julia and Crown Prince Rashid of Tamir are to marry after all. Today's announcement by the palace marks the end of one of the most tumultuous royal courtships in recent memory. After rejecting three of Prince Rashid's proposals publicly, and an unknown number privately, Princess Julia has finally agreed to the union.

Both families are said to be delighted with the outcome. It was apparently made possible by the resolution of the mystery surrounding the deaths, over a century ago, of Prince Omar Kamal and Princess Delia Sebastiani. The story is to be turned into a film in the first-ever Montebello-Tamir joint arts project, it was announced.

The wedding will be private, the *Messenger* has learned. The family does not wish to mount a formal state celebration while questions about Prince Lucas's fate are still unresolved.

Epilogue

Bells rang with delight all over Montebello as Julia and Rashid came through the church doors into the bright island sunshine. Out in the square thousands of waiting citizens sent up a deafening cheer. From somewhere nearby a cloud of white balloons went up. Sirens blared, horns sounded.

The royal couple stood for a moment just outside the high arched entrance, while cameras clicked and hummed and the cheering swelled and burst.

The prince was heart-stoppingly handsome, dressed with all the traditional magnificence of Tamiri princes. Wearing a gold-embroidered, dark blue silk high-necked jacket and flowing white *shalwar,* he was swathed with ropes of fine pearls over his chest. At his hip hung a curving scimitar in a richly jewelled scabbard. On his fingers were several gold rings, embedded with large precious stones—emerald, ruby, and sapphire. And on his shining black hair a blue silk turban, the ends sweeping over one shoulder to give him a somewhat piratical air, was draped with more pearls and a massive, gleaming diamond.

But no jewel matched his eyes, glowing with possessive pride as he looked down at his princess bride.

Julia, more beautiful than ever in a creamy white silk brocade dress and veil threaded with a latticework of pearls and diamanté, seemed caught in a net of sparkling light. Her bouquet was a tumbled mass of exotic blue, purple and white flowers. On her smooth bare throat was a beautiful sapphire necklace that was King Ahmed's gift to his new daughter-in-law, as were the magnificent sapphire drop earrings.

Her eyes glowed with blue fire and when she turned from waving at the crowd and the cameras to smile up at her new husband, everyone saw how he caught his breath. He took her hand in his.

"My wife," he murmured, and drew her hand to his lips. The crowd roared its approval.

After a few minutes the royal pair was joined by the rest of the wedding party. The four bridesmaids, Nadia, Samira and Leila Kamal, and Anna Sebastiani, came out of the church first, along with Christina Sebastiani Dalton, who was matron of honour. All wore varying shades of blue to tone with Julia's tumbled bouquet. With them came Hassan, his brother's best man.

King Marcus and Queen Gwendolyn, along with King Ahmed and Queen Alima, came out of the church chatting together, and provoking a renewed wave of cheering and flag-waving from a populace thrilled to see with their own eyes this evidence that the tensions between their two countries were dying. Everybody knew that talks would be beginning soon between the two monarchs, with a view to building closer ties and bringing firm peace between Tamir and Montebello.

For a few minutes, as the guests spilled out into the sunlight after them, the Sebastianis and the Kamals stood on the grass, milling and chatting like any ordinary families on a day that marked their union, and at least as happy as their subjects that the long feud was finally over.

As their wives stood apart, talking about the moving ceremony just past, in which a mix of two traditions had been achieved, King Ahmed and King Marcus were left on their own together. They stood facing each other for a moment of awkward silence, and then shook hands. Then, as if this reaffirmation of the male bonding mechanism encouraged them both, they clapped each other on the shoulder.

The cheers behind them practically tore the leaves from the trees.

The two fathers turned and stood shoulder to shoulder watching their newly joined offspring standing in dappled sunlight chatting with well-wishers. Julia's pregnancy was just visible under the snowy silk of her dress.

"They make a striking couple," King Ahmed said. "*Insh'Allah*, the child will inherit the throne of Tamir, in due course."

"Let's hope the day is a long time coming," Marcus responded in automatic diplomacy.

Ahmed bowed. "And you—will you make him your own heir? Will the boy sit on the joint throne of Tamir and Montebello when his moment arrives?"

Marcus's lips tightened. "I make no decisions about an heir at present. As you know, there has been no final word on my son, Lucas," he said. "Miracles have happened before this, and my wife and I are praying for one."

Ahmed bowed again. "May Allah answer your prayers, my friend."

Across the lawn, Julia and Rashid now formed a laughing group with Nadia, Christina and her husband, Jack.

"It seems fairly obvious," said Nadia after a few minutes of banter, "that you two owe your present happiness to Christina and me! Where would you have been without our sisterly advice and concern?"

"Absolutely," Christina agreed solemnly.

Rashid grinned at his sister. "I'll have to return the compliment one day soon."

The happy laughter made the little square ring. Soon, however, Rashid turned to his bride and slipped an arm around her waist.

"Shall we?" he murmured. The bridal couple led the way down the path to the ranks of white limousines and slipped inside as the cheers of the crowd rose to a roar.

One by one the limousines and cars filled up and left for the short journey up to San Sebastian palace, where the reception was to be held.

When the square was quiet again, and the crowd and the television crews were dispersing, when there was no one to take particular notice, five men came out of the church and moved down the walk together.

A few people still in the square turned and gazed curiously for a moment. There was something about the five men that drew the eye. Perhaps it was the air of deep connection between them, so that, if they had not all been physically so individual, you might have guessed them to be brothers. Their comradeship was palpable, as was the sense of their having been through terrible challenges together, and survived.

Perhaps it was some quality they all shared. A sense of honour, perhaps. Or integrity.

No one in the crowd recognized the men, and yet there was some magnetism that drew the eye. If someone had said to those who watched, "These men have been called the Five Noble Men," no one would have been surprised.

Gordon Hunter, Edward Ramsey, Jonathan Dalton, Caleb Stone and Richard Sutter stood together for a moment as the last limousine silently moved to the curb and stopped in front of them.

"Well, the boys seem to have done all right," said one. The others nodded their agreement.

"Better than we could have?"

"It's a pretty comprehensive solution, isn't it? Marriage, peace negotiations, the terrorists given a crippling set-back...and each of our firstborn sons has found himself a bride. Did any of us guess how much change this mission would bring about?"

They laughed together, their greying heads tossed back in the brilliant sun, and the years fell away. The few watching blinked, for just for one moment they seemed to see the men as they had once been, handsome young warriors, laughing together because, through courage, and cunning, and luck, they have survived the unsurvivable.

The moment passed, and the men bent one by one and slipped into the limousine. Then doors slammed, and the car moved away, and the little churchyard returned to the silence of its centuries.

*   *   *   *   *

*Be sure to watch for Alexandra Sellers's
next breathtaking story!*
THE PLAYBOY SHEIKH,
*a Silhouette Desire MAN OF THE MONTH
and the next installment of the*
SONS OF THE DESERT *miniseries,*
will be available in February 2002.

Rumors abound that the missing
crown prince of Montebello
is still alive!
Will Prince Lucas Sebastiani be found?
Don't miss the exciting search in
ROMANCING THE CROWN,
a brand-new twelve-book continuity!
The search begins with
THE MAN WHO WOULD BE KING
by Linda Turner (IM1124),
available from Silhouette Intimate Moments
in January 2002!
And if you'd like to read
a brand-new short story
featuring the royal families of Montebello,
look for *ROYALLY PREGNANT*
by Linda Turner,
available right now
from Silhouette Books in the anthology
CROWNED HEARTS
Turn the page for a sneak preview of
ROYALLY PREGNANT...

Chapter 1

She wasn't there.

Rafe searched in vain for the wavy, shoulder-length curls of the slender blonde who had haunted his dreams for the past six months.

Dammit, where was she? he fumed. He hadn't been able to get her out of his head since his cousin Julia's wedding, and that irritated him no end. The last woman who'd captivated his thoughts so completely had turned out to be a money-grabbing little witch who broke his heart, and he'd sworn then that he'd never fall in love again. And he hadn't.

But damn Serena had tempted him. She hadn't been anything like the debutantes who hounded him wherever he went, smiling at him so prettily while they plotted and schemed to become his duchess. Introducing herself simply as Serena, she'd wanted nothing from him but a dance. And when one dance had led to another and they'd eventually escaped to his room for an incredible night of lovemaking, she'd slipped away before dawn the next morning without even leaving him a number where he could reach her. And he'd thought of nothing but her since.

She'd bewitched him—there was no other explanation. He knew it, accepted it and for months had looked forward to this New Year's ball at the palace so that he could see her again. And she was nowhere to be found.

"Who is she?"

Caught up in his thoughts, he hardly heard his cousin Anna's question. Frowning, he jerked his attention to her and found her watching him with narrowed eyes. "What?"

"The woman you're looking for," she replied. "Who is she?"

A proud man, Rafe couldn't tell her or anyone else about Serena and the way he still ached for her six months after a single night of loving. Not after she'd left him before dawn without a backward glance. So he forced a smile and shrugged. "I don't know what you're talking about."

Not fooled, she arched a mocking brow. "Really? I thought you might be looking for the blonde you were so taken with at Julia's wedding."

"What blonde?"

She laughed. "Just because you don't see her doesn't mean she isn't here. Guests wander all over the palace. She could be anywhere. You should look around."

"There's no blonde," he said stubbornly. "I was just looking over the crowd. I heard Julia Roberts was coming with my brother Drew tonight."

"You're not kidding, are you?"

"Of course not," he said innocently. "I wouldn't do anything like that."

They both knew he would do exactly that, but she obviously couldn't take the chance. "I'd better go find

Mother. She'll be thrilled she's coming. She loved her in *Erin Brockovich.*''

Excusing herself, she hurried away, and Rafe found himself separated from his bevy of admirers by the crowd on the dance floor. Taking advantage of the situation, he slipped outside.

The second the French doors closed behind him, shutting out the sounds of the party, Rafe sighed in relief. The beauties inside wouldn't follow him—not when it was so cool and dark clouds overhead in the night sky threatened rain—and that was just fine with him. He needed some time to himself.

Alone with his thoughts, he felt the quiet shadows of the palace's extensive gardens beckoning him into the night. His mind once again wandering to Serena, he took one of the garden's many meandering paths and soon left the party far behind.

When lightning flashed overhead a few minutes later, revealing a woman on her knees digging among the roses at the far end of the garden, Rafe thought his imagination was playing tricks on him. For a split second something about the way she moved reminded him of Serena.

''You're seeing things,'' he muttered to himself. ''If she was here, she certainly wouldn't be working in the garden!''

Then, with a loud crack of thunder, lightning flashed again, lighting up the night sky. Startled, the mysterious gardener rose unsteadily to her feet and half turned toward him, giving him a clear view of her silhouette. Shocked, Rafe froze in his tracks.

It was Serena. And she was pregnant.

**Take a walk on the dark side of love
with three tales by**

For centuries, loneliness has haunted them from
dusk till dawn. Yet now, from out of the darkness,
shines the light of eternal life…eternal love.

Discover the stories at the heart of the series…

TWILIGHT PHANTASIES
TWILIGHT MEMORIES
TWILIGHT ILLUSIONS

Available December 2001 at your favorite retail outlet.

Where love comes alive™

Visit Silhouette at www.eHarlequin.com   PSWITN

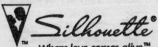